NOTHING FALLS

FROM

NOWHERE

Stories

by

GARY FINCKE

Production Manager: Kimberly Verhines
Copy Editor: Mallory Lecroy
Cover Design: Meredith Janning

IBSN: 978-1-62288-405-6

For more information:
Stephen F. Austin State University Press
P.O. Box 13007 SFA Station
Nacogdoches, Texas 75962
sfapress@sfasu.edu
www.sfasu.edu/sfapress
936-468-1078

Distributed by Texas A&M University Press Consortium
www.tamupress.com

Contents

To all the grandchildren:
Gavin, Raea, Sabina, and River

Nothing Falls from Nowhere

<u>Tim</u>

Like she always did when we traveled to New York City, my wife Sally drove the Ohio leg from where we lived near Cincinnati. Our daughter Christine took over at the rest stop just inside Pennsylvania. Route 80 from there into New Jersey was long, but easy. They relied on me to do the last 100 miles, half of that in heavy traffic no matter that it would be after midnight when we neared the city.

Which was why Christine was driving and me half asleep in the back seat when the windshield exploded in the middle of Pennsylvania. Christine screamed and braked hard, but it was Sally who took the rock full in the face. I sat up and leaned forward and wanted to scream myself. For all of the blood, I didn't know where her face was, but I could see her brain.

<u>Wesley</u>

Randy and I had an hour to kill waiting for my big brother Luke to get off work. We stopped at the DQ so we could have chocolate cones without Luke making fun of us, and after Randy turned off onto Well's Hollow Road, I let out a whoop because I knew what was coming, him plowing into Max Wagoner's corn and bumping along taking the full-grown stalks down. We couldn't see shit except all those stalks slapping at the windshield like those rubber flappers do at the car wash, and then we were out the other side away from the Wagoner house so even if he heard the car or saw our headlights, we were way too far gone for him to catch us.

Randy drove almost to the Turkey Hill before he pulled over and we picked out the leaves that were stuck in the grill and inside the fenders. If he noticed any of that, Luke would tell us that was old shit we needed to leave behind and call us pussies as if being eighteen and out of school two months made him King Daddy.

We cleaned that car good because Luke didn't say a word about us being kids, but when Randy said we should throw rocks off the Route 80 overpass, I thought Luke would tell him to grow the fuck up. Instead, he said "Cool," and we stopped where we knew a farmer smarter than old Wagoner had plowed stones out of his field and left them near the highway to keep guys like me and Randy from driving through. We each took three. I kept mine softball size and so did Randy, but Luke had three that could have passed for bowling balls pretty near. "These motherfuckers will break some shit," he said.

Christine

Dad told me later that I screamed until he got off the phone, but that can't be right because I heard everything he said when he called 911. I had the car stopped and off on the shoulder by then, and he was saying, "This is bad. A rock broke right through the windshield. It just crashed in from out of nowhere. My wife's struggling for her life. My God, half her brain is gone. Oh, my God."

Later, when somebody from the newspaper talked to the dispatcher, she said she could hear somebody screaming the whole time my father was on the phone. Like my voice was caught on tape for some kind of evidence.

Wesley

I threw my rocks as far as I could, and none of mine hit anything but Route 80. Randy aimed real careful-like at oncoming cars and didn't hit a thing. It was Luke who hit a truck with his second stone, and we high-fived after it bounced off the hood. "Give this big mother a heave," he said. "Let's see if one of you pussies has grown some hair."

Randy gave me a shove in the back, and I half stumbled. "Fuck you," I said, but there it was, that heavy thing that was hard to do anything with except throw it from just off my shoulder like I was shot-putting. When we heard the windshield shatter, all three of us hollered and laughed. Randy even did a little dance instead of getting right into the car. I had to yell at him like he was going to stay there and celebrate until the cops showed up. All the way to my house he kept saying, "You hear that? You hear that? Fucking awesome." When we got to the house, Luke had to tell him to shut the fuck up.

Marvin

I heard the boys come in around midnight. They knew I'd be at the tv, so it wasn't like they had to sneak in. With my wife Leah dead and buried going on a year, I'd taken to watching a movie after the news, something to keep company with until I could settle enough to sleep. My job at the mall ended at ten, and I'd gotten into habits— getting up late, eating lunch instead of breakfast, not caring my own self about the extra pounds.

But when they seemed all keyed up, opening and closing the refrigerator, looking through the cupboards like scavengers, I waved at the tv and told them I was going to bed. "You boys help yourself," was what I told them. "Play your video games or watch a movie. Just stop all that hunting and pecking in the kitchen and remember this isn't a bar the next time you open the refrigerator."

Tim

Sally had just finished speaking with our boy Rick before the rock struck her. She asked him to send her a selfie from where he was stationed in Texas. "It's only a week before you ship out," she said. "I need more pictures."

The picture came through and Sally showed it to Christine, who looked at it so long I had to tell her to keep her eyes on the road. "I really miss all you guys," he texted.

"He's so sweet," Sally said. She put the phone in her purse and the rock burst through.

Marvin

I heard the boys leave and looked out to see my car gone. I heard them come back and leave again. I drifted off for a bit and came right up straight in bed when I heard the doorbell.

The sweat came right out of me. I checked the boys' room and saw their beds empty and wished to Christ I'd come out and locked them up for the night the second time they'd come back, even that little wingnut Randy.

There was nothing for it but to open the door to the police and, as it turned out, be thanking God when the officer told me that a car had been damaged on the freeway, nowhere my boys would be. I blew out a breath just before the cop added, "A passenger has been seriously injured."

"You think somebody lives here is involved?" I said.

"We'd like to find out. There's a car in your driveway was seen twice driving past the scene. We find that unusual."

I looked and there it was, my car back where it belonged. Randy's was there, too. "They must be around here some place," I said.

"That's what we believe, sir," the cop said, and just then all three came up from the basement so I knew they'd snuck in quiet as church mice and gone down there to filch beer straight from the case like I wouldn't count.

Doctor Wentworth

There was every chance trauma like the kind the woman had suffered from being struck by the rock would be fatal no matter the effort that was made to save her. But even as we worked on her, hours upon hours, everyone in the room had a sense of how extensive the repairs would be, how many more operations we would be sharing before she could have any hope of leaving the hospital. She could very well be dissatisfied with her diminished quality of life. I'd seen cases less terrible than hers where the ongoing treatment created an uneasy balance between gratitude and cost. Not only the financial. That was the easy part.

Randy

It was Wesley's idea to go back to check things out, but it was Luke who said, "I'll drive," and I knew right off he thought I'd screw something up, stall the car right on the bridge or pull over to take a look down with the cops there like they had to be by now. But when he got into his Pop's car, I thought maybe it was Wesley he was worried about, what he might be thinking about the damage all that glass breaking might mean.

So we just cruised by slow, and Wesley piped up, saying, "Look at that, the staties are here too."

Though when I said, "This'll be famous," I got a look from Luke like I was a total moron.

Marvin

From the very first, when I studied on what the paper had to say about it, I expected the woman to die, one son turning to killer, the other an accessory. Like werewolves, they'd be in the papers, when she went. Brain surgery sounded like something doctors did to say they'd tried. Taking off the top of her head. It sounded like what they did for those boxers who get their brains beat in. Duk-Koo Kim, Kid Paret, and all the rest like them, though if I told my boys they'd just look at me like I was making things up. Nobody follows the fights anymore. The kids, for sure, don't know a thing except their cartoon fights they're all the time playing.

Doctor Wentworth

There are times, while operating, that I think anything can not only be corrected, but also made new. A perfect orbital reconstruction. A seamless cranial prosthesis. Things Sally Kirsch would need when she came out of her induced coma. If the stone had crushed her face thirty-five years ago when she was her daughter's age, she almost certainly would have died, and had she lived, her face would have broadcast her deformities like neon. I had a friend whose mother went through a windshield around that time, her lacerations leaving scars that transfixed people and made her keep to herself for the rest of her life, something to remember each time I stand over a patient like Sally Kirsch who had already lost an eye, whose skull cap I'd removed to allow for swelling in her brain. And when I read the newspaper accounts two days after, I noticed that one of those boys swore that every rock he threw hit nothing whatsoever, as if a shooter missing his target is a synonym for innocence.

Marvin

My boys both took the blame for the rock that hit the teacher's car. Some comfort in that, though I admit I wished all along that it was Randy who'd tossed the accurate one, that my boys would be guilty because they were dumb enough to keep him around instead of the other way people would be seeing them now, Randy spreading the word about how he didn't lay a hand on that stone, and if egged along a bit with a smile or two and a handy lawyer, drifting into saying he didn't know what he was doing out there on the bridge until he was watching rocks crashing among speeding cars, hitting a truck and then the car with the teacher from Ohio. If I had to do it myself, I'd take an oath and swear his hands were covered in clay dust, that I'd heard him bragging about being the one with the idea, the one who'd thrown the first stone.

Wesley

"What does that mean, Pop" I said, "an induced coma?"

Pop just looked at me and said, "What do you think it means?"

I studied on that a few seconds until I thought I had it worked out. "They put her to sleep, and she won't wake up unless they let her."

When Pop nodded, I said, "That don't make sense. Aunt Bev was in a coma until Uncle Ray had them pull the plug. A month she laid there, and she didn't change at all."

"This lady's not Aunt Beverly. There looks to be different kinds of comas." He squeezed my shoulder. "Ones that maybe people wake up from, maybe feeling better than you might imagine."

Randy

They had all of our names in the paper, all in a row like we'd done the same thing like some kind of circus act. Luke and Wesley Walters, Randy Osgood. I got credit for one thing that was right, driving my Mitsubishi Eclipse when we stopped on the overpass near Route 80's Midway Exit. But then there was this—"When the car below them slowed, they fled to the house where the brothers lived." We didn't flee. We just knew to celebrate somewhere else. Bank robbers do the same thing. They don't flee, they escape.

There was this, too—"They tried to watch a movie, but dying to know how much damage they'd caused, they got in the Walters' gold

Honda Accord and drove past the scene to see what was happening." How does some reporter know what we we were dying to do? If he'd asked me, I'd have told him I was dying to get Bonnie Roenig into bed, and I didn't much care where.

But I'll admit to the one thing—that second trip back to look yet again? That one's on me. All those extra police cruisers meant we'd done more than break a windshield, and there was the Honda's license plate in plain sight.

Tim

When I read in the newspaper what the trucker who was hit right before us said, I thought he was grandstanding. The fuck it happened like that, a thump like thunder, the rush past of something big and heavy like a meteor. And now here he is up for getting himself in the papers as the luckiest guy and all that goes with it. There's vanity everywhere was what I thought, even among misery.

Christine

Every year, Mom has an individual picture of each of her students on a kitchen bulletin board. They're arranged to coincide with where they sit in her classroom. From time to time she switches a few—because they talk too much maybe, but more likely because she's learned one of them has trouble seeing the black board or one has a hearing problem uncorrected. She wants me to see them when she tells stories during dinner. So you know who I'm talking about, she says. To help you understand.

Now school has started with a substitute, and my mother's students could be sitting anywhere. They could be disrupting class, switching seats without permission. Or one of them might be squinting from the back row, too ashamed to let that substitute know she can't see a thing.

Randy

I told the cops it's about wrecking things, not hurting anybody, but they looked like they wanted to slap my face or maybe more. Everybody I know hits mailboxes with ball bats. Everybody does a corn run, even girls sometimes. It's not like we were out drunk driving and being way stupid.

Doctor Wentworth

Two weeks in an induced coma is exactly what Sally Kirsch needed. The body needs time after thirteen hours of surgery to save its life and reconstruct its face. It was the worst case I'd ever seen, and nothing since has changed my mind.

Wesley

Pop was always telling me, Luke too, that Randy was so squirrely he was trouble waiting to happen. Twitchy is what I'd say. Like the alien monster was inside him and fixing to get out. Pop let us watch that movie when I was eleven. "You're about grown," he said, "and it's better than having you sneak it behind my back." He'd bought it used someplace, but the whole way through, Randy acted like he was six or something, pissing his pants for every little scary thing. Pop called him Ripley after that even though she was the strongest one in the crew. He said he coud tell Randy had a girly side. For a while it was funny. And then Randy got big enough to whip me, so what did that make me?

Christine

Dad's told me about the trucker and his meteor. "My ass," he said. "If it bounced away and didn't hit you, you'd think it came from right here on Earth. Afterwards you'd know you could drive out there and pick up that rock and never once think it was anything except something pulled from the ground."

There's always the talk about meteors hitting us head on, ending us once and for all like the dinosaurs. Those guys with their telescopes can see them coming for a million miles so they'd know way before us we're all going to be disintegrated. And then they'd have to tell everybody, and there would be fighting back and forth about whether they had it right. They'd be like weathermen predicting a hurricane. People would hope that path might change. Them and their prayers and such. But it makes me think on what would you do once it got to where the end of everything was a sure shot. It's what movies are made of—heroes and cowards and those who turn to a few weeks of pure evil because it's been in their nature all along.

Wesley

Pop was all the time thanking the doctors for saving me from murder, but sometimes I wished that lady was dead right away. She'd have been gone then instead of all the time looking at me with her one eye half blind in her smashed up face. She's like some kind of ghost everybody loves. Like Casper for old people—they all want to give her a hug.

Marvin

During the winter when Wesley was twelve, he searched the sky for the first sign of space junk that was forecast to tumble out of orbit. "What if it lands here?" he asked more than once, and each time I told him that was so close to impossible there was no sense thinking about it. "But not 100% impossible, right?" he said,

He asked to sleep downstairs in the room where we kept an old bed for when relatives visited. From time to time I caught him walking with his eyes focused on the sky. "Will we be able to see it coming?" he asked, and when Leah said, "Not likely," he had her go outside with him with binoculars. He worried more on cloudy days, but by February he knew that the space station would break apart and mostly disintegrate before it reached Earth. Still, he wouldn't let it go. "So many pieces make it worse," he said.

The space station plunged back to Earth one night when nobody within five thousand miles of us noticed a thing. Wesley, he acted disappointed, like he wanted that pile of junk to land on the Johnson property right next door.

Wesley

Mom was nice about it the winter I was scared of space junk falling on us. Pop said stuff like that always fell in the ocean so don't be such a baby.

I looked space junk up on Mom's laptop. In 1962, a twenty-one-pound metal object plummeted from the sky and landed at the intersection of two streets in Manitowoc, Wisconsin. It turned out to be part of Sputnik IV, the first piece of space junk surviving re-entry after falling out of orbit. The part I wanted Pop to see was it ended up imbedded three inches deep in the asphalt street.

Pop told me to shut the computer off and do something useful. "There's no point in being afraid of something you can't fight," he said.

Doctor Wentworth

A titanium implant is an extraordinary thing. The skull discarded, no longer viable, yet medical science permitting the body to re-enter the world.

Randy

It wore me down, all the talk about prison and me knowing I hadn't even touched that rock the Walters boys almost killed somebody with. I considered on some regrets I could have, but after a while, as part of a plea deal, I agreed to testify against Luke and Wesley. They would have done the same if I hadn't got first in line is how I figured. Luke always made fun of me, and their Pop thought I was some kind of handicap. "Ants in your pants" is what he always said like he'd just thought of it after saying it since forever.

And I didn't lie. That's what's important. There's nothing wrong with telling the truth like I did in these exact words: "We decided to throw rocks at cars, just go out and be bad. When we got to the overpass, Wesley and Luke jumped out of the car with rocks ready to go. By the time I was up there beside them, Wesley had tossed a rock so there was no going back like maybe we could have done if they wasn't in such a hurry to put a hurt on something. For absolute sure, I didn't hit a thing. But there was a loud crash when Luke's rock that Wesley tossed hit glass. We all laughed as we drove away."

Wesley

"We're not a bunch of retards," I told the lawyer Pop got for me and Luke. It's just chance. And such a long shot. I knew twenty guys who'd thrown stuff off that overpass—rocks, sure, but also golf balls, and even old books. Sometimes they hit cars, but never a windshield, not with rocks at least. The lawyer didn't even write it down. He looked bored. Like he wanted me to make something up. A good lie instead of the truth.

Marvin

The police questioned Ron Davenport, who lives only 100 feet from the overpass. He mentioned to them that kids had tossed rocks at tractor trailers from the same bridge about seven years ago. "Then they put the signs up, 'No standing on bridge,' and there for a while the cops were coming by on a regular basis checking. But nothing happened, so the cops stopped coming by."

Tim

When asked by the reporters, the state police said they didn't know how many times someone threw an object that struck a vehicle last year, because its database lumps those in with incidents in which something lands on a highway. What they knew was troopers responded to 213 "assault-propulsion of missile" incidents last year. What else they knew was fences are erected on highway overpasses in urban areas that have sidewalks and are near a school or playground. The Willow Hill Road overpass where those boys threw from doesn't meet that criteria because it's in a rural area, with no sidewalk. The overpass, they said, is twenty-two feet high.

There are dozens of stories of rocks thrown from overpasses. Near misses, mostly, but one man, driving near Austin, was hit square in the face like Sally. He ended up paralyzed on his right side and unable to talk or write. Think that's one of a kind? Three other motorists were injured in rock throwing incidents on the same highway within a month of the one that paralyzed that driver.

Marvin

I told this story to Leah way back when and to my boys once upon a time, but now it sounds like I'm the devil talking to say it:

One afternoon, just after recess ended, a corner of concrete from under the roof of my elementary school broke off and fell fifty feet into the playground. Our teacher kept us in our seats. She told us to pay attention to what we were doing, not what was happening outside, but when school ended, everyone I knew stopped to take a look at the crash site. We all said we remembered exactly how long it had been since we had stood in the spot where the stone struck the cement. Last week. Yesterday. That morning. Minutes before.

Doctor Wentworth

When I was fourteen, I went with friends up the winding outside staircase that led to the top of the water tower at the county park. We had water balloons, balancing two in each hand. "There's always somebody who doesn't know enough to not stand around close to the tower," one friend said, meaning other people who were there for our church picnic. By the time we reached the 100-foot-high observation deck, I was uneasy with the height and having only one way down after we tossed those balloons. My friends screamed when a balloon burst close enough to somebody to soak them. I was the only one who didn't lean over the railing to see the damage. Before the last balloons were tossed, I made my way down the stairs and hoped that anyone coming up the metal steps would figure I wasn't part of the group that threw the balloons, that anyone soaked would see me half way down while one last balloon arced toward them.

Christine

Nearly three months it took for Mom to leave the hospital. Dad spent half those days in Pennsylvania. He made me go back to Ohio State for my sophomore year, and I put up with sympathy that started to smell like too many flowers in a room.

Tim

I learned that two drivers were killed by rocks as big as soccer balls tossed onto a German highway in 2000. Like the boys who hit our car, all of those rock throwers were teenagers. They were charged with murder.

Christine

In November, while we were waiting at the rehab center for Mom's grand exit, one of the nurses told my father and me about the time in 1969 a big cloud formed out of nowhere over Chester, South Carolina. "Right away powder started to fall all over that place and the people were afraid," she said. "Nearly all of them went inside and closed their windows. Some who were stuck outside expected to die. But it turned out to be from the new Borden's plant. It was the stuff they make to put in coffee."

"Cremora," Dad said. He knew the name right away.

The nurse looked surprised. "The person who told me didn't know the name," she said.

"Some people down that way got to be happy for a bit thinking the world didn't fall on them," Dad said.

"Dad, Mom's alive," I said. "She's coming home."

"Yes," the nurse said, "isn't that wonderful?" and she hurried away.

Doctor Wentworth

When Mrs. Kirsch stepped out of the Medical Center for the first time since being struck, she wore a pink #KirschStrong t-shirt. Her artificial skull was covered by a pink and white knit cap. Outside the rehab facility, she was filmed ringing a victory bell reserved for patients who overcome long odds. When she first entered the facility, she was so confused she couldn't manage any of the therapy. Three months since the incident, she said she had no memory of it. Anyone watching the video will notice that as she walks, Mrs. Kirsch is braced on both sides by smiling attendants. At the victory bell ceremony, she is still lightly supported. When asked to speak, what I said was she was "nearly independent, walking with a little assistance, able to take care of herself."

Christine

My mother came out of the hospital like a prisoner, her exposed eye blinking. She wobbled when she paused at the applause, the hands of two aides on her shoulders. A woman next to me checked her phone, and my father's head snapped sideways to glare, his mouth working the way it does when he's choking back curses. For a moment, the day began to lose its balance, and then my mother took a few tentative steps unaided, and my father put his arm around my shoulders and drew me close as everything straightened and held steady.

Tim

Everybody looks happy in the video of Sally's release, and so do I. But they're all like Christine, not thinking about having to live the rest of what's coming without being swallowed. I can be angry, but

I can't say a word about being uncomfortable. I'd be a selfish prick if I let it slip how her face isn't hers anymore, that it belongs to the doctors and the rock throwers.

One of the reporters volunteered this: "Where I come from, those boys would be afraid for their lives when the word got out about their stupidity."

I didn't ask her where that was, but if she was making that up to lead me along, I was willing to go. "There's some of that in me," I said. "That's one way of how some might handle such a terrible thing."

Christine

My father said, "There will be times you wish her dead." He refused to believe me when I said "never."

I waited a long time for him to snap out of it and say "Sorry" or "I didn't mean that," but he finally said was, "You'll see." Just like that, without inflection. Like it was a sentence for which there was no appeal. Like there was nothing that would surprise me, that anything could fall from nowhere.

Marvin

"You're good boys," I told them right after the teacher went home to Ohio at last. Luke paused the movie he and Wesley were watching, and I readied myself to accept their bodies in a hug. "You sure are," I went on, "don't let nobody tell you different."

They shifted in their chairs, but neither stood. On the screen, an actor who was aiming an arrow at an enormous dragon. I'd seen this before. So had the boys. The outcome was impossible, but it was about to happen, and what came to me was wondering whether either one of them would have paused the movie if he'd never seen it before, whether his eyes would have stayed on that dragon, his head nodding, while I finished what I had to say and left the room.

Tim

All of us have a life sentence. My daughter will lose her hope. My son will feel like he's been redeployed.

Marvin

My Wesley, he needs to be tried as a juvenile, him being sixteen at the time. That's something to feel better about, the lawyer said to me. And he wanted me to know there was certain evidence he wanted to be suppressed when the trial rolled around. Most important, he said, is not to admit as evidence the 911 call made by Mr. Kirsch. Likewise, pictures of his Missus should not be permitted to be shown. They're prejudicial, he said. Those exhibits are too emotionally charged.

Christine

My mother has a new skull. Like a crab entering a new shell. And now my father and I will examine the crease of its circumference as often as we enter a room where we find her. She will pretend not to notice until one day my brother will be back from Afghanistan all in one piece, and my father will give up a smile and we will fix on her whole body, believing it will go on by itself. We will feel some small sense of what might be happiness, all of us thinking the same thing, "Here we are, here we really are."

The Faces of Christ

UNTIL I WAS THIRTEEN AND WAS ALLOWED to go with friends, I thought everybody went to the movies like my parents, walking in whenever they arrived, seeing whatever happened to be playing from half way through or from near the end or beginning, then staying until the part where they came in.

I didn't mind. The good news was we went to the movies every Friday night except when my father worked three-to-eleven, going to see whatever was showing in Factoryville. We didn't get a newspaper. We just drove into town and picked one or the other of the two theaters. "Ok," my mother would say. "Look up the street and tell us what's at the Penn."

EVEN AT FIFTEEN, I STILL LOVED THAT MOMENT as our Chevy crossed the intersection. Depending on the title and the size of the lettering, there were nights when I could shout out the movie at the Penn before my father could spot the title on the marquee at the Factory, which was two blocks farther down Industry Avenue. Horror movies and gangster films were what I watched with my friends, and for our family, there was always a costume drama or a western, a musical or comedy.

Or most important, a Bible epic, because, for sure, if Jesus was in a movie, my father picked that one every time. *The Robe*, for instance, when I was in first grade. And the sequel, *Demetrius and the Gladiators*, even though it was second-hand Jesus, since he'd already been crucified in *The Robe*.

My sister Linda and I knew the stories, of course—how they'd turn out-- so no matter what miracles he performed, Jesus was always going to ride the donkey into Jerusalem and get hung on the cross. "It's no different than Shakespeare," my mother would say. "You know what happens to Romeo and Juliet and Julius Caesar and all the rest."

My sister, thirteen, didn't get it, but by now I'd read those two plays in school—we did one Shakespeare a year--and that was exactly the problem. It was just like Shakespeare, and I wasn't looking forward to *Hamlet* and *Macbeth*. I'd had about enough of these people talking to each other like nobody had ever talked in the history of the world. I wanted stories where the characters had a million little problems instead of one enormous one. Like I did. The way I felt like I was walking in a cloud of gnats. I had to keep fanning the air around my face or I'd be swallowing the things or squeezing them out of my tear-filled eyes.

And to tell the truth, Jesus was never exactly in those movies, because he was only shown from the back--long flowing hair, a white robe, a set of hands meant to display character by being folded in prayer or lying gently on top of someone's head, especially a child's or a sick person's. And he always had a beautiful, soft, warm voice speaking the King James or Revised Standard English of the Bible.

Worse, we were supposed to know Jesus was the son of God from the awestruck look on the faces of disciples and crowds of people in drab robes. When he reached the important part of what he was saying, he became outstretched hands and an uplifted back of the head, intoning advice in the perfectly pitched voice of the Messiah because seeing the face of Christ on screen was blasphemous.

But shortly before Christmas, the year I was in tenth grade, we saw *King of Kings*, arriving during the Beatitudes, and suddenly, before we'd even settled in, there was Jesus looking right at us. The Son of God had blue eyes and was pretty-boy handsome because he was being played by an actor named Jeffrey Hunter who I'd seen in *The Great Locomotive Chase* with my friend Ken Lester.

"That was worse than nudity," my father said in the car five minutes after Jesus, facing us, started preaching "Blessed are" for the second time.

"When did we ever see that?" I said, but my father didn't answer.

"I don't think your father wants to talk about it," my mother said, and he didn't, at least not until Sunday when he stopped at a newsstand after church, something that surprised me because we kept the Sabbath holy by never doing anything, not even buying a paper, since that required someone else's work.

"It's not enough they made that fellow Jesus," my father said. "He acted like he was just an ordinary human being. Nobody would believe that a Jesus who walked and talked like that had anything to do with God." He stared at the newsstand through the side window, said "I'll be back in a minute," and returned with the Sunday edition of the *Pittsburgh Press*.

Half way through lunch he opened the newspaper to the entertainment section and started to read. "The movies always play in Pittsburgh before they play in Factoryville," he said. "I'll know what's coming next time."

"Ok," my mother said.

"We have to be careful now," he said. "There's no telling what's next."

ON MONDAY, RON FRANKEL, WHO SAT BEHIND ME in home room, brought his record to school. "I recorded it over Thanksgiving," he said. Frankel carried the 45 with his finger crooked through the hole. The paper sleeve had the same texture as the bags I carried my lunch in. *U U U Records*, it said on the top of the label. Underneath the hole, it said "I Know You're Dreaming," Rolf Kranen, 1:55.

"Get it?" Frankel said.

Nobody standing outside of homeroom said anything until JoAnne Fernald breathed "Ohhhh" and smiled the way she did when I fantasized her in my bedroom. Frankel twirled the record three times before she said, "It's an anagram."

"Is that the same as a stage name?" Darlene Gillis said, but I'd been working on decoding U U U, and by now I knew what that song would sound like. My mother had shoved nickels into a jukebox and listened to "You, You, You" during every lunch we ate in a diner the summer before I started first grade. Every time I ate a hamburger or a hot dog, I heard the Ames brothers singing it.

"Rolf Kranen. It makes you sound like Troy Donahue," JoAnne said. "Can we hear it?"

"Wednesday," Frankel said. "Miss Sohlman said we could use her record player at the end of class when the Twentieth Century is over."

"It's about time it ends," Darlene said. "She's been playing those records since school started."

In history class, Miss Sohlman had a record player she used near the end of every lesson. Since October, she'd been playing *Twentieth Century Voices on Record*—an eyewitness giving a live broadcast of the Hindenburg Zeppelin burning, Roosevelt delivering the "fear itself" pep talk, Lou Gehrig declaring himself the luckiest man alive even though he was dying, and just last week, Nixon giving his "Checkers speech." Monday afternoon, when we were finished listening to Jonas Salk announcing the end of polio, she told us the only speech left was Kennedy's inaugural address. "And then Alan Shepard's flight," Miss Sohlman said. "History has caught up to us. Think about that. If we'd heard this record at the beginning of 1961 instead of at the end, Kennedy wouldn't have spoken yet, and we'd still be wondering if that rocket would fly."

There were two minutes left before the bell, enough time for Miss Sohlman to talk about movies, her favorite subject, but Ron Frankel put his hand up to ask why there wasn't anything on that record about the concentration camps and the Nazis. "Well," Miss Sohlman said, "this is American history."

"The concentration camps are part of American history," Frankel said.

Miss Sohlman walked toward the door as if she was going to lock it. "We don't have those voices recorded."

"Because everybody kept their mouths shut," Frankel said, swiveling in his second row seat to look at the rest of us. "Think about that the next time you need somebody's help."

"There were men," Miss Sohlman said, "who thought they were killing people who were different out of love for people like themselves." The bell rang, but all of us waited because Miss Sohlman took a deep breath. "That's unforgivable," she said then. "That's what hell is for."

"Jesus Christ," Ken Lester said while he rummaged through his locker after school. "Frankel thinks we're all ready to kiss his ass and listen to history after class is over just because of his stupid song. I bet it's shitty. Frankel doesn't even look like somebody who could sing. He looks like a fairy. He looks more Jewish than Miss Sohlman. What's he think—all those questions about the Nazis will raise his grade?"

"He'll look different if people think he's Rolf Kranen," I said.

"Frankel's been telling us about this record since school began," Ken said. "How he wrote a song, how he was going to record it. You see him twirling that record? Now he expects us to listen to him tell us about how hard it is to be a Jew."

"That UUU on his record is for the Ames Brothers song," I said.

Ken slapped his locker shut and clipped the lock together. "What are you talking about, Gene?"

"'You, You, You.' Remember that song from when we were little?"

"No." Ken left his jacket open even though it was thirty degrees outside. "He'll be bringing a stack of records to sell in school, you can bet on that," he said. "That Jew-boy wants our money. The girls will buy for sure."

The wind flapped Ken's jacket wide open as we walked toward the bus. "You ever see Frankel's parents picking out a tree at the place where you work?" he said, laughing. I shrugged. I was making a dollar fifty an hour waiting for people to choose a Christmas tree, and then it was my job to help them tie it to their cars. A dollar sixty-seven, really, because for the first six nights I'd worked, Mr. Sheffler, who sold the trees from an empty lot beside his house, had given me five dollars, saying "For good measure," each time.

"A BOY YOUR AGE WOULDN'T REMEMBER that old song," my mother said, when I brought up my record label theory at dinner.

"I do," I said. "I could sing it right now."

"Spare us," my father said, opening the *Pittsburgh Press* as my mother slid pieces of pie onto small plates.

"I'll tell you what I do know," my mother said. "That boy sounds like he has money at his house. No fifteen-year-old gets to make a record unless he lives with somebody who can pay."

"Paul Anka was fifteen when he made 'Diana.'" I said. "Richie Valens was sixteen when he started."

"Isn't Richie Valens dead?" my sister said.

"Well, yes," my mother said slowly, as if I'd made an important point. "That poor boy is gone, but Paul Anka was cute. Is this boy at your school cute?"

"Not really."

TUESDAY AFTERNOON WE HEARD KENNEDY SAY, "Ask what you can do for your country" again. "Now that these are almost over," Miss Sohlman said, "we'll start having longer current events sessions." She glanced at the clock, but she didn't move from beside the record player. "President Kennedy has just sent troops to a country called Vietnam. Does anybody know what Vietnam used to be called?"

"It says on the ditto sheet he sent military advisors," Ken said, pointing to the hand out Miss Sohlman gave us each week.

"You boys should keep up with this," she said, but when the bell rang, we didn't wait to find out another name for Vietnam.

"How boring can one class be?" Ken said in the hall. "The only thing about current events that's interesting is The Twist."

"It'll be interesting tomorrow," I said. "Frankel gets to play his record right after Alan Shepard blasts off."

"Good," he said. "Then history and Frankel will both be over. You can bet nobody will do The Twist while Frankel's singing. We ought to break that record. We ought to crack it over his head."

"Not until we hear it at least," I said. "If it's bad, the girls will laugh and he'll want to break it himself."

That night my father opened the newspaper as soon as he sat down for dinner. My mother watched as he folded it and laid it beside his plate. "Maybe there won't be any more Bible movies for a while," she said.

"Maybe."

"Maybe you don't have to do so much research. We can just go to whatever's playing this Friday like we always do." She lifted a bowl of mashed potatoes and extended her arm toward him, but my father tapped the folded newspaper. "Listen to this," he said. "Somebody in Mississippi says she saw the face of Jesus on the refrigerator on the porch of her neighbor, and now there's people by the thousands driving by to see for themselves."

"Why's the refrigerator on the porch?" I said.

My mother set the bowl down and sighed. "Some people live that way."

My sister looked at my father. "How do they know it's Jesus?"

My father rapped the paper against the table as if he'd spotted a crawling bug. "Maybe they went to that movie we saw, and now they think they know."

My mother spooned potatoes onto her plate and mine. She poured gravy over them and added slabs of roast beef, leaving the platters so close to her my father would have to ask if he wanted anything but the green beans that sat untouched in the middle of the table. "Ron Frankel's playing the record he made tomorrow," I said.

"Nobody needs another rock and roll song," my father said. "A priest in this story says it's a miracle. The Catholics are always seeing things."

"I'll bet it's better than you think," I said.

"A boy your age is singing. It can't be good."

My mother nudged the green beans my way. "Unless he's Paul Anka," she said.

My father turned the newspaper over, then unfolded it to where the movie ads for Pittsburgh were. "Pick one of these," he said to my mother. "I'm changing shifts, so we'll have time before. We'll go someplace different this week. Maybe do some Christmas shopping in Pittsburgh."

My mother pointed to a picture of Hayley Mills. "This one," she said. "It has that perky girl in it. The one who's Gene's age." When my father didn't answer, she said, "You remember *The Parent Trap*, don't you, Larry? You laughed all the way through it."

My father nodded. "That girl?" he said. "Good." My mother smiled at my sister as if they'd planned to go to see Hayley Mills all along.

WEDNESDAY, AS PROMISED, WE HEARD the countdown and Alan Shepard saying, "Light this candle." After he blasted off, we waited for the splashdown and a voice to announce Shepard was out of the capsule, and then we sat up because it was time for Ron Frankel to play his record.

Frankel fiddled with the dials like he was launching a rocket himself. Everybody knew it was just left for treble and right for bass, that the one other knob barely turned up the volume before the speaker started to vibrate.

Finally, he lifted the arm and set the needle down so slowly I thought his homemade record didn't have that little wide space at the beginning. There was a short crackle, a piano riff—da dah, da dah, da dah dah dah--and then Frankel singing, "I know you're dreaming of me when you're wide awake."

It was corny and the drums were too loud, but I saw the girls were entranced, all of them looking at Frankel as he mouthed the words like he was on American Bandstand—"You want me, I know you do. You need me, I know you do. You love me, I know you do."

The song ended by repeating the opening riff, the piano slowing and growing soft. The class, except for Ken, applauded. I put my hands together once and held them there while I watched JoAnne Fernald clap as if it added points to her grade.

"Who do you think Frankel's thinking about when he sings?" Ken asked after school. "You think maybe it's a boy and not a girl? He acts like such a fairy."

"Come on," I said. "Frankel carries rubbers in his wallet just like we do."

"But he doesn't use them."

Neither did I, but every month I changed my rubber to another brand in case somebody checked. There weren't any locks in gym class. I knew Ken was the kind of guy who looked.

"Let me ask you this," Ken said. "If Frankel wanted you to go to the movies with him, would you go?" I thought for a second, and Ken smiled. "See?" he said.

"I didn't say *no*."

"Sure you did. Just now."

Right before we turned the corner toward the door, we passed Frankel's locker. He'd pasted a sign on the door that said, "On Sale Here—I Know You're Dreaming--$1"

"Listen," I said, "I'm going back to talk to JoAnne, maybe bring up the Christmas dance."

"You do that," Ken said. "Ask her before Frankel asks you."

I shrugged and started walking. I could hitchhike home. It didn't matter that I wasn't allowed "because you never know," according to my mother. Even with a ten-minute lead, that bus would stop and start so often I'd catch up in time to keep her from finding out. Frankel would sell me one for a dollar. All I had to do was ask. Open my mouth like I did at the dentist, and then make it move.

When I came back around the corner, I saw that Frankel had his locker open, that he was taking dollar bills and passing out records, eight of them while I watched, including one to JoAnne. I felt the three wadded dollars in my pocket, but I didn't pull any of them out. "You going to enter the talent show?" JoAnne asked him, and I shuffled closer.

"That would be a step backwards," Frankel said.

"Elvis lost his high school talent show," I said, moving up beside them as if somebody wanted to hear what I knew.

"Really?" JoAnne said, looking my way.

"That's what I heard."

"Wow," she said, and then she followed the other girls toward where the buses waited.

Frankel watched them as he closed his locker. "So you know," he said.

"What?"

"The UUU is for Elvis. You knew right away I twisted up Elvis' lines, all the `yous' from "I Want You, I Need You, I Love You.""

"I thought maybe," I said, and Frankel clicked his lock and spun it as if I might want to know the last number of his three-number combination. I backed up toward Miss Sohlman's room, acting like I had somewhere to go.

"Well, you were right, but I used UUU as a sort of tribute to show I wasn't just stealing."

"It's ok," I said, but I turned and walked through her doorway, leaving Frankel to either walk or hitch a ride home on his own. Miss Sohlman looked up from her desk, and the first thing I blurted was, "Before now, was there ever a movie that showed the face of Jesus?"

"Did you go to *King of Kings*?"

"Yeah. My father acts like it's the end of the world or something."

Miss Sohlman smiled. "You tell him the face isn't important, that the story is about betrayal and cruelty and horror. You tell him stories like that teach us what's coming unless we learn to take care of ourselves."

"He acted like it was the first time ever."

"It's happened before, Gene. There was a movie a few years back with a Jesus from the front. It was called *Day of Triumph*."

"Really? We must have missed it," I said.

"You didn't miss much. The man who played Jesus was way too old for that story."

THE NEXT MORNING, IN THIRD PERIOD BIOLOGY, I counted six girls who had Frankel's record between their geometry and biology books. Joanne was one of them, and the only reason I could think of was she'd brought it back to get Frankel's autograph. I nudged her geometry book, trying to see more of the record. She was my lab partner because her name was next to mine alphabetically, but I hated coming to lab right after gym class. Boys had five minutes to shower and dress, and I was always still sweating. Girls had fifteen minutes. I checked the clock when they went downstairs after doing something called rhythmic gymnastics—throwing streamers around, twirling hoops, tossing beach balls. At the other end of the gym we played basketball for half a day of bragging rights.

"You know what's on the other side?" JoAnne said, and I reached for the microscope, a drop of sweat splashing onto the lab table.

"No idea," I said, putting my eye to the lens.

"Nothing," she said. "Do you think I got a bad copy? I brought it back in case."

"No," I said, and then I stood up straight, slid the record from between the books, and smiled at the blank side as if it showed JoAnne coming down the stairs of her house in her Christmas dance dress.

"THE STUDIO WHERE THE RECORD was made is on the North Side," I said at breakfast on Thursday. Linda was gone, but I was still at the table because I had the morning off for a dentist appointment. "It's on the same street as Dr. Murray's office."

My father grunted from behind the Pittsburgh *Post-Gazette* he was holding, half-folded, with one hand. My mother shook her head.

"Your father's buying the morning paper for a while because he's working eleven-to-seven."

He lifted the paper again, and I looked at my mother. "You make sure you brush your teeth," she said. "You don't want Dr. Murray finding your breakfast stuck between them."

By the time I came out of the bathroom, my father was standing beside the car. "Get in," he said. He drove down East Ohio Street as if he always took me to the dentist instead of never; he sat waiting for me in Dr. Murray's office while I had tartar scraped off my teeth and spit blood into a little bowl where water never stopped bubbling.

"Ready for television," Dr. Murray said to my father as he paid.

"Not this one," my father said. "Radio. Rock and roll."

"American Bandstand." Dr. Murray said.

As he shoved his wallet into his work pants, my father stared at Dr. Murray. "Pittsburgh basement," he said.

Outside, I motioned my father past the car. "Can we look for a minute?" I said. "There's only a couple of blocks."

He fixed his eyes up the street as if he was deciding how many blocks were in "a couple." "If it will put an end to this," he said.

Six doors down, we turned into Strother's Music and Studio. "You think Frankel's record is for sale in here?" I said.

"Not hardly," my father said. He tapped on a glass countertop until a clerk turned our way. "Can a person make a record here if he has a mind to?"

The clerk nodded toward the back of the store where a short, skinny bald guy was sitting on a metal stool beside the classical music shelves. "Ok?" my father said, but I was thumbing through the popular 45s, looking through the Ks for Frankel's record. He gave my coat a tug at the collar and pulled me toward a row of album covers that featured tuxedoed men playing violins.

"Your boy want to make a record?" the man on the stool said.

I shook my head. "So modest," my father said. He gestured at the door marked STUDIO. "How do you work this?"

The man pushed himself up and opened the door. "These kids come in. I figure they can't do much worse than what I'm hearing every day walk out of here, so here I went and opened up a little studio in the back."

My father looked at me. "Well?" he said, "you want a look-see?" The store had put carpet on the walls and the ceiling. It was like we were upside down. Our voices, surrounded by carpet, seemed thinner, the way Frankel's did on his record. In the center of the room were a drum set and a piano. "They bring the rest if they want it," the man said. "All it takes is a tape recorder better than the ones they play with in high school. We can do echo effects, make them sound like they're singing in a cave." He waved us toward the center of the room. "Don't be shy on my account," the man said. "There's a place that presses records for me. By the hundred, you know. The kids decide how many. They're like senior pictures. They can trade them, sign them--you know, you have a boy there."

My father acted like he was waiting for something. I swallowed and walked around like I wasn't thinking of anything but designing a studio myself. "Was Ron Frankel recording here three weeks ago?" I finally asked.

The man shook his head. "Not that I recall."

"How about Rolf Kranen?" I said.

He looked puzzled. "What kind of name is that?" he said.

A minute later I stopped on the sidewalk outside Strother's and stared down the street. "You think there's another studio around here?" I asked my father.

"Why not?" he said. "Everybody's a singer these days."

In the car, I told my father that Frankel hadn't used any echo on his record. "Good," my father said. "Then he at least sounds like himself."

The business district disappeared behind us without another studio sign. "Miss Sohlman told me she saw another movie with the face of Christ a few years ago," I said.

My father stared at the car in front of us. "Miss Sohlman? With a name like that, what would she be doing at a movie about Christ?"

I DIDN'T SEE ANY RECORDS IN NOTEBOOKS that afternoon. I didn't see Ken Lester either because he was absent. Frankel's sign was still up, but he was standing by himself as I walked toward him after school. I fished a folded dollar out of my black chinos and handed it to him, catching myself looking up and down the hall as he reached inside his locker and pulled out a copy of "I Must Be Dreaming."

Frankel looked pleased. "You're the first guy to buy one," he said.

That night, when Mr. Sheffler asked, like he did every night, how school went, I told him I went to the dentist so it was better than usual. He laughed and said, "Now you're ready for your close up."

Just before nine o'clock I helped a man tie one of our largest trees to the top of his car while his three small children watched. Mr. Sheffler put his hand on my shoulder and smiled as the car disappeared. "You're a perfect helper, Gene." I felt his hand tighten a bit before he lifted it. "I mean it. In every way. Come inside the house. I have something extra for you. It's getting close to Christmas. You can buy your girlfriend something really nice."

"I don't have a girlfriend," I said, and he feigned surprise.

"Really? A boy your age?" he said, opening the door. "How do you satisfy yourself?"

I stopped just inside the door, pretending I hadn't heard him, but Mr. Sheffler took a step closer. "You know. You're what? Fifteen? You must need to satisfy yourself every day."

I couldn't think of an answer that didn't sound like a lie. I tried to remember whether I could reach the door if I extended my arm behind me. "How does this look to you?" he said. Mr. Sheffler held out a twenty dollar bill, and I waited for him to say he didn't have change, that he'd pay me next time or something, but he stared at me and said, "I can pay like this every time if you give me some."

"What?" I managed, but I swallowed hard and felt my face get hot.

"You know what I mean. Give me some," and he put his hand with the twenty dollars in it on my belt buckle, slipping it open and tugging at my zipper. I closed my eyes. I stood there and felt my jeans and boxers slide down past my knees, and then I heard him say, "Oh yes" just before he put my penis in his mouth and I began to stiffen.

When I finished, Mr. Sheffler stood up and said, "See? It's just like being inside a girl." He kissed my forehead, his lips so warm and moist I shuddered.

I WROTE AN EXCUSE FOR MYSELF for Friday's gym class, saying I'd had two teeth pulled, and I wasn't to exert myself because the stitches might pull loose. Mr. Brady tossed it onto a pile and waved me to the bleachers where I silently repeated my vow to ask JoAnne to the dance as soon as I walked into biology because for once I wouldn't be sweaty and almost late.

I was so early to biology there were only four students in the room as I waited by the door. Walking toward me, JoAnne was wearing a light blue sweater that was softer looking than any piece of clothing I'd ever touched, and I slid into the doorway, saying, before I lost my nerve, "Would you like to go to the dance with me?"

"Ok, Gene," she said at once, but I didn't feel happy like I thought I would. It was like I was making up for letting Sheffler blow me.

"Great," I said, and then a crowd of students pushed past us, and I didn't have to say anything else for the rest of the period because Mr. Larson always lectured on Fridays.

EVEN THOUGH IT WAS BETTER THAN ANOTHER NIGHT in Factoryville, I didn't want to go to Pittsburgh. "Mr. Sheffler already has a boy for Fridays," my father said. "If you're not working, you come with the family."

"You'll like this one, Gene," my mother said. "*Whistle Down the Wind*, it's called. And I checked up on Hayley Mills. She's not only your age, she was born in April, just like you. You're practically twins."

Linda smirked. "Hayley Mills would never go out with Gene."

"Why ever not?"

Linda paused as if she was gearing up for something special. "He's too weird," she said.

There was a crowd in the lobby of the theater when we walked in, but my father worked his way through it to the entrance. An usher stood behind a velvet rope. "May I help you?" he said as my father approached, and when my father looked puzzled, he added, "The next seating is in nine minutes."

"Come on," my mother said, "come away from there," tugging his sleeve.

So for once we sat through the previews before we saw even one minute of the movie, which started off with Hayley Mills opening the door to a barn and finding a man with long hair and a beard. "Who are you?" she said, and the man muttered, "Jesus Christ."

I glanced over to see how my father had taken to swearing so early in a movie, but it wasn't long before I could see swearing wasn't the half of it. I could tell we were supposed to think maybe the guy with the beard and long hair was Jesus, and that maybe only kids like Hayley Mills and her friends would believe in him.

After a while it even seemed like Hayley Mills would do anything the guy with the beard wanted. My sister sat between me and my father, but I could hear him whispering to her, and finally he stood up, and Linda tugged on my arm. "Come on," she said, standing up. And when I saw my mother was on her feet, I had to get up and slide sideways past six people to the aisle.

I followed my father from the theater. "That's the last time for that," he said, and I knew he'd decided to stop going to the movies altogether, that somehow the world had changed into a place where "worse than ever" was a certainty.

"What will they think of next?" he said to my mother. I had an answer for him, but he walked in front of us then, head down, with my sister beside him, both of them moving so fast they were half a block ahead of us by the time we reached the car.

"He'll get over it," my mother said, but I was sure she was wrong.

SATURDAY NIGHT I WAS LATE FOR WORK, walking the half mile to Mr. Sheffler's so slowly it was 6:10 when I arrived. "Hi there," Mr. Sheffler said as if he didn't mind.

I said "Hi" and got to work. I kept busy with customers, and when nobody was around, I moved trees, fixing things to make it look like all the ones that were left were trees people should buy rather than scrawny ones nobody wanted.

No matter where I was, though, every time the customers thinned out, I saw Mr. Sheffler watching me. Finally, just before nine o'clock, he acted like he was rearranging the leftover trees near me. "How did that make you feel the other night?" he said

"I don't know," I said, and as soon as I heard those words in his pleased expression, I added, "I quit," and started walking the half mile back to my house. I didn't need the five dollars I wouldn't get. I was already ahead with the twenty, and now it didn't seem like I'd been paid so much extra.

ON THE NEWS, JUST BEFORE WE GOT HOME from church the next day, the announcer mentioned synagogue vandalism. "The swastikas were seen by passing motorists."

"Of course," my father said, "nobody else would be around today," and my mother drew in a hiss of breath.

He glanced over at her as we reached our driveway. "You know those swastikas will be on the news for a week," he said. My mother sighed and reached for the door handle. "And don't you go huffing and puffing about something you know is true."

During lunch, I asked my father if he'd found the swastika story in the newspaper. "No," he said.

"That paper gets printed before midnight," my mother said. "They wouldn't know about the synagogue in time."

"Well, they're lucky it's a Sunday. They don't have to honor the Sabbath, so they don't have to worry about whether to scrub walls all day."

I pushed my chair back, stood up, and said, "I can walk on Sunday, can't I?"

"Sure you can walk," my father said. "Who said anything about walking being work or play?"

"I'll see you later then."

My father glanced up. "Should I be calling some boy's parents in an hour to see what you're up to?"

"I don't know," I said, looking back from the door. "Maybe I'll hitch a ride to Pittsburgh to see how the movie turned out."

I stepped out fast, then, closing the door and heading across the just-sold farm that bordered the road to Frankel's house. It was nearly a mile, but I had my head down and my arms swinging, and fifteen minutes later I could see him standing beside a dark blue Chrysler in his driveway. "Hey," I said, trying to sound casual. "Was that your church on the news?"

"That's where we're going," he said. I noticed Frankel's father sitting at the wheel. "To clean all that scum off."

I watched as his mother and his younger brother stepped out of the house. "I'll go along and help if you have room," I said to her.

Frankel opened the door for his mother. "Sunday's your day of rest, isn't it?" she said.

"No, not really," I said.

She rested one hand against the doorframe. "You want to call your parents? This could be hours."

"It's ok. They're busy with something else." Mrs. Frankel nodded and slid inside the Chrysler. "Ronald's friend is coming along to help clean," she said to her husband.

At the synagogue I saw two policemen standing near three empty cans of paint and three white-stained brushes. "Maybe they can find out who bought those," Mrs. Frankel said. "There's ways."

Mr. Frankel handed me a brush and a bucket of warm, suds-filled water. "At least they were dumb enough to use paint you can scrub off with soap," he said.

Frankel and I stood side by side scrubbing at a pair of large Christmas stickers that showed a nativity scene. I didn't say anything until I'd erased every part of the wise men and the shepherds, and then, when I moved toward the nearest swastika, one that looked like it was drawn wrong, I said, "You going to see *Judgment at Nuremberg*?"

Frankel reached up and picked away at the baby Jesus. "What's that?" he said.

"A movie. Miss Sohlman told me about it. It's about the trial for old Nazis."

Frankel kept picking. "My parents don't go to movies—they read."

"Miss Sohlman really knows movies. She goes to everything."

Frankel's sticker was gone, and he moved closer, ready to take on the swastika beside mine. "I'd like to think of a good reason to talk to her like that. You ever look down her blouse when you're standing at her desk?" he said.

I started on the broken swastika, wiping and scouring. The hard-bristled brush had a place scooped out where a hand fit. Somebody had meant for that thing to be gripped tightly for serious work.

I took off that crooked swastika and thought about Frankel wanting to stand over Miss Sohlman, and it seemed to me there was no way of telling who was who unless something happened you could see with your own eyes. For all I knew, right after we'd left the movie theater, the guy with the beard might have healed somebody. I hoped so. And I hoped my father would keep his vow never to go to the movies again because I never wanted to sit beside him and worry whether or not something was going to happen on the screen that made him squirm.

An hour later, I heard Mr. Frankel say, "We're about done with this wall. There's a bad patch off to our left by the street." Ron glanced at me, but I kept on with what I was doing. If they came back here to inspect after they finished the bad patch, they'd pitch in and help. If they didn't, I could clean up by myself. All I had to do was scrub off five small swastikas and a Jesus head one of the vandals had taken the time to paint.

I decided to leave Jesus until last, but half way through the first swastika, I caught myself singing Frankel's song. "You want me, I know you do; you need me, I know you do; you love me, I know you do." Maybe, I thought, if you didn't see Frankel singing it, it could be a hit. You could find somebody who looked like Bobby Vee or Bobby Rydell to mouth the words, but you couldn't get Elvis because he'd have to know right away where that song came from.

I stepped back from the wall, making sure that the swastika outline was completely gone. The last four swastikas looked like they'd been drawn by an expert. But when I took a look at Jesus, I thought the vandal should have skipped the swastikas and drawn only the face of Christ turned away, just painting long hair, both arms upraised, a flowing robe. People would have gathered, trying to guess whose hair and arms were on the wall. For sure, my father would have made fun of the crowd that gathered, reading the story to us during dinner. And then he would have driven here the same way he'd driven to the Catholic Church to see all the Nixon bumper stickers somebody had pasted up before the election the year before. He would have walked around, moved forward and back, changing the angle and distance, knowing, at last, that if this head turned, Jesus would be looking him in the eye.

Delightful Conversation

When Dakota opened the door of the small house set above the river, Trevor Kantz extended his arms to hug her, but she backed away and said, "Touching don't seem right for this here." Trevor had been braced for hysteria, but it didn't take long to recognize the standoffishness she'd shown him ever since he'd introduced himself to her as Travis' gay brother. Travis had warned him, but he'd wanted to get past that right off. He'd even made a little joke about himself, saying "unemployed," "skinny," and "gay," as if all of his adjectives about himself were equally self-deprecating. She'd have room to maneuver, he'd thought, but she'd said, "Is that so?" in a tone that so heavily emphasized contempt he thought it covered all three qualities, what with Travis holding down a computer job, her being about 5'7" and weighing maybe 170 by the looks of it, and Travis announcing they were getting married.

Travis had said, "Two of those are in the process of changing. Baby brother has an interview next week, and he's eating like he wants to catch up to me." Travis weighed 230 then, going soft, but at six-four not somebody you'd imagine gaining fifty pounds within a year after getting married. And Dakota was tall enough at the time to pass as a woman some would call voluptuous.

Trevor had laughed. He'd tried "Two out of three ain't bad," as if an old Meat Loaf song could speak for him. Dakota, for her part, had looked him up and down like she was trying to identify the symptoms of the disease he'd just announced. And from then on, she'd stayed tight-lipped around him, her sentences brief or reduced to clipped phrases and single words. Even more likely, silence.

What else he didn't expect as she let him enter the house was how carefully she was dressed. Hair styled, makeup, the expensive gold necklace Travis had given her on their first anniversary. "The paper was here this morning," she said right off. "I have this on because I wanted to look good for Travis. Somebody has to hear his side. Look at all this they're saying."

Trevor looked to where she had the morning local paper spread out on the kitchen table. There were two paragraphs about how Travis' body had been found in a raggedy-looking lot on the same block as a house he owned and seemed to have been fixing in Riverton. There were three paragraphs about how Travis frequented the strip club a few miles south of Portview, where he lived with his wife. And four paragraphs of comments by a stripper who said she felt bad because Travis was such a nice guy. Like a biography, Trevor thought. An unauthorized one.

"They're making him out a crazy person full of secrets," Dakota said. "It's not crazy to fix up a house so you can rent it and make money. It's not a secret if you sit at a strip club in plain sight. Secret and crazy are all the men who look at porn all day on their computers with the door locked."

Dakota grabbed the other sections of the newspaper and balled them up before tossing them into the wastebasket. "Stabbed repeatedly," she said. "How many fucking times is that? When is it more than several times? It's like he was butchered." She paused, gasping, and Trevor nearly reached for her again before she took a breath and added, "Like he's nobody at all. Like an animal." For a moment, she went quiet, her breathing back to normal, and then she said, "Thank you for coming, but I need you to stay someplace besides here if you're staying for the funeral."

"I already have a room," Trevor said. "I figured as much."

THE MOTEL WHERE TREVOR HAD RENTED A ROOM was the kind where men pay by the week or month. He'd worked in the motel's restaurant when he was in high school, short-order cooking on weekend mornings when the place filled up with locals as well as the overnight guests. Twenty years since then, but he'd had a burst of nostalgia seeing the place still in business. But now, returning to the room at nine o'clock after nursing a few beers in a restaurant with central air, he concentrated on examining the dripping air conditioning unit in the window and noticed that something like stalactites had formed beneath it. When he turned it on, he imagined the fundamentals of Legionnaire's disease in every breath. He decided to run it for an hour while he walked. Maybe whatever cold it worked into the room would last until he fell asleep.

Hiking along the highway's shoulder was harrowing, the traffic on the four-lane road heavy. A half mile of facing oncoming trucks, and he settled for going into Dunkin Donuts. He ordered two crème-filled, what Travis always bought, but he left the second one on the plate after taking one bite, dumping it in the trash. He bought a bottle of Lysol spray at the convenience store a hundred yards farther up the highway and used it to clean the sink, the mirror, the floor of the shower and the toilet seat, telling himself the expense and the time was a sort of tax on memory.

The room was cooler, at least, though he had been quick to turn off the air conditioner. He stripped to his boxers and held the pillow to the light, examining it with his eyes and nose. Passable, he told himself, but when he heard a door slam in the next room after he lay down, he felt so vulnerable that his heart raced.

A loud chatter of Spanish began, and he was grateful, at least, for his end room because the thin wall admitted a crowd of voices, enough, he guessed, to account for four men sleeping two to a bed. He tried to imagine their jobs, what paid for their miserable room, and when there was a burst of laughter, he came up blank for what might make them happy. Already the warmth had regathered, and all he could do was throw off the yellowed sheets.

WOKEN BY THE HEAT, HE WAS UP BY SIX, out the door within half an hour. There wasn't a car outside of the Spanish-speaking room. None anywhere within five rooms. The restaurant, he'd been told the night before, had closed three years ago. When he opened the newspaper to read with his Egg McMuffin, orange juice, and coffee, he recognized Dakota's outfit, but the photograph was on page three, her interview underneath it because an eighteen-year-old girl had been arrested for the murder, her picture and story on the front page and continued on page two.

How many killers are caught before the funeral of the victim? Trevor thought. *School shooters, wife beaters, sure, but the rest?* But here she was, the knife already found that stabbed his brother twenty-two times according to the article that called it a thrill kill, a man a few years older hiding behind the front seat in case she ran into trouble finishing the job.

"You never know what's in peoples' hearts," the police chief had told the reporter. "That's why the police are always busy."

The girl, apparently, wasn't denying anything. Her only excuse was that Travis had started groping her as she was driving toward some place where she could kill him in private. "I didn't know he'd be so big," she said. "I started getting afraid with his hands on me and him looking like 300 pounds at least." *The stupid cunt*, Trevor thought, forming the phrase with his lips, imagining saying the words out loud. Since the wedding, Dakota had grown fatter than Travis. Lately she'd made the two of them together weigh more than 500 pounds. A quarter ton— the weight sounded like the payload of a small pickup truck.

TREVOR SPENT THE MORNING DRIVING to every location mentioned in the article. The mall parking lot where he'd met the girl, the strip club that he frequented, the block with the empty lot where his body had been found, the house two doors away that Travis owned, the house where the crazy girl and her boyfriend rented three upstairs rooms. After lunch, he drove back to Portview.

This time he found Dakota in tears. "That bitch makes Travis sound obese. Travis weighed 285 and was tall. They don't even mention his height anywhere. Those that don't know him will think I was married to a pig."

"The bigger he sounds, the less guilty she is."

"Somebody needs to correct her, make her tell the truth."

He knew she was twenty-nine, eleven years younger than Travis, something that diminished any excuse she might have. "I knew he loved me," she said. "He said it every time he left the house. Every time. Never missed."

Trevor nodded, feeling like a policeman.

"Craig's List. I thought it was queers who hook up with strangers. No offense," but he didn't change expression or answer. Let her be, he thought, no matter what. "Isn't that what goes on at the video store up that way and farther up there in the county park. Everybody knows." She shifted her weight, the chair creaking. "Well?" she said. "It's all true. You don't have to say anything." She folded the front section of the newspaper, smoothed it. "She said she was somebody who supplied 'delightful conversation.' The fuck. Everybody will think Travis a fat fool and a scumbucket both."

"Everybody will know she said it that way to protect herself," Trevor said. "Plenty of respectable people answer those ads."

"And plenty not," Dakota said. "You know, Travis always worried about you and your risks, what you'd run into. He said queers always cheat on their steady guys."

"Except me," Trevor said.

"Really? How about Neal?"

"Him too."

Taking a deep breath, Dakota pushed herself up from the chair, walking to the living room window as if she'd heard something outside. "It's the damndest thing, isn't it," she said. "Hardly more than a girl. Already a mother, to boot. If it wasn't in the paper, who would believe it?"

"Probably nobody."

"Sandy from next door is making me dinner," Dakota said. "She's been helping with arrangements. I know you just got here, but I'll see you tomorrow."

THERE WERE UPDATES ON THE FIVE O'CLOCK NEWS Trevor watched in his motel room before he took his second shower. The girl has admitted that she and her boyfriend celebrated by going to a strip club, using the money they'd found in Travis' wallet. What he was going to pay her with, Trevor thought, but just then the next-door Spanish revved up again, and when Trevor stepped outside, deciding to drive to Panera Bread before heading down along the river to the strip club, there still was no car anywhere near the rooms closest to his.

He'd pulled into the strip club parking lot the day before, sitting among four cars in full daylight, but after dinner and a long walk in the residential neighborhood behind Panera, it was nearly dark, and he counted sixteen cars.

Inside, he asked the man who looked to be a bouncer if the woman who had spoken to the newspaper about Travis was working. "Maybe," the man said, and when Travis asked again, "maybe not."

"The man who was murdered, the one she talked about in the newspaper, I'm his brother," Trevor tried.

"You don't look anything like that fat fuck. Maybe you're just the police."

"You know his name, right?" Trevor said. He opened his wallet and showed him his driver's license. "See?"

The bouncer lifted the wallet from Trevor's hand and squinted. "She's on in half an hour. I'll see if she's willing. Buy a few drinks. Make everybody glad you came."

Trevor ordered a beer, finished it, and ordered another. There was nothing to do but watch the bare-breasted woman who was on stage working the glittering pole only a few feet away. One more beer, he told himself, before he became a fool. He kept his eyes on the woman and tried to put himself in his brother's place, feel his desire as some pop song he didn't recognize blared.

He remembered the old Van Halen video Travis loved for "Hot for Teacher," the teacher in a blue bikini swinging around a pole. It reminded him of high school when he followed the cues of his friends, the signals for laughter, and how he'd been afraid every day that he'd be found out.

And it called up, like it always did, that moment in the kitchen at work, when he'd realized, talking to a boy his age who went to a Catholic school, that he'd met someone he might share more than small talk with. Their joy in each other and relief that they went to different schools, the accidental secrecy they kept for nearly a year until he'd come out at graduation.

Just as he ordered a third beer, a woman wearing a loosely tied robe over a sparkling bikini approached and sat down, talking immediately. "You're his brother? Really? I have to admit you take care of yourself better than he did, but you sure act like a cop the way you've been sitting there pretending to have fun for twenty minutes."

"I'm trying to know all sides of him. There's a little cop in that, I guess."

"You never went out with him when you hung out?"

"Not to places like this."

She looked at him. "You're gay, right?"

"Yes."

"Your eyes are always up here," she said, pointing to her face. "It's a thing I don't run into much, even the cops eyeball your tits. They act like they're off at a distance, but their eyes grope you the whole time."

"I can imagine."

"Your brother was a good tipper, if that's what you want to know. He liked it all. 'Delightful conversation'—who does she think she's kidding? That house of his he was supposed to be working on. It has furniture in it, I bet."

"I wouldn't know."

"Listen. You know what he'd say to me? I looked like his wife would if she lost 100 pounds. I felt bad for him."

"He had his own to lose."

She stood, the robe flowing open, and Trevor looked beyond her. "You going to stay and watch?" she said.

"No," Trevor said, but when she started to turn away, he pushed himself to his feet and looked into her eyes. "That girl who stabbed him said they went to a strip club to celebrate."

"Maybe down toward Harrisburg then. I was on that night, and those two weren't in here," she said, and it felt like some small comfort to Trevor that they'd driven past here, that they hadn't celebrated in his brother's neighborhood, something that would have linked where the body was tossed to where he lived. He hoped that they hadn't known anything about Travis, that he hadn't talked about himself as that girl drove toward Riverton, that he'd revealed nothing of himself but bad judgment to his killers.

LATE THE NEXT MORNING, READING THE NEWSPAPER with breakfast at Perkin's, Trevor inhaled a bit of the fat blueberry muffin that came with his eggs and ham. He coughed for a minute, sipping juice to settle himself. "You ok?" his waitress asked, though when he nodded, she didn't leave. "You had me scared there for a moment," she said. "It reminded me of my father choking with his esophagus cancer. How he wouldn't eat in front of anybody after a while. All the time with the throat clearing and then the spitting in a cup like a tobacco chewer near the end."

"It's just me being careless," Trevor said, but he could see the place was nearly empty, that no help from other tables needing something even as she leaned over the table and pointed at his open newspaper. "Those two stupids," she said, "trading a few days on the front page for a lifetime in jail."

"It looks that way," Trevor said. He lifted his fork, but she didn't budge.

"Anybody with brains would wear their best I'm sorry face and calm things down."

"They're already about as worst as worst can be," Trevor offered, and then he shoved a bite of cheese and spinach omelet into his mouth as a period.

"We can only hope. The creeps. It's like they want to be a tornado, but all they are is a nasty little squall."

When she didn't walk away, Trevor swallowed and said, "It's my brother who got stabbed."

She gave a quick little forced laugh. "No way," she said, and Trevor pushed the entire last quarter of the huge muffin into his mouth, working it into a wad of paste as she backed up at last. "Oh," she said, but by now she was beyond the neighboring table, and Trevor had forced the muffin down his throat.

SANDY ANSWERED THE DOOR when Trevor knocked. "She said you was going to show up and to tell you she's down in the dumps today."

"I can stay or go," Trevor said. "Whatever's best."

"If you ask me, she's embarrassed like she oughta be what with all the shenanigans on top of the tragedy." Sandy folded her thick arms below her breasts, her body nearly shapeless in her loose dress. "You likely know about such things what with your proclivities and all."

"How's that?"

Trevor regretted not walking inside as soon as the door opened. Now it felt as if he'd have to shove Sandy aside if he wanted to enter. "Nothing," she said, but a smile worked its way onto her face. "At least you didn't bring your pal along."

"Neal's been out of my life for quite some time now."

"Which kind of queer are you?" she said. "You the boy or the girl when you're doing your business with Neal?"

"Top," he said, regretting, at once, that he'd answered.

"Well, that's some word to remember for when I try to picture it, but let me tell you if you wasn't blood kin to Travis, I'd bring my boy over to kick your ass right off this here porch."

"He built like you?" Trevor said, and when her expression turned uncertain, he felt a flash of pleasure that blinked out when he saw Dakota standing in the hallway looking devastated.

Sandy followed his eyes and turned. "Your faggot's here," she said, but Dakota waved her hands in front of her face as if a swarm of gnats had materialized. Dakota, Trevor saw, was crying, but now she walked into the living room and stood with her hands on her hips.

"The death notice runs tomorrow morning. The funeral's in the afternoon."

"Well then," Sandy said. "I'll be sure to buy a paper, and I'll leave you two to commiserate."

"That wasn't about you," Trevor said, but when Dakota looked beyond him, he turned and saw that Sandy had stopped a few steps into the yard.

He took a step inside so he could shut the screen door, but Dakota didn't move. "I know better," she said, "but Sandy thinks she's only a couple of weeks without pizza and ice cream from her high school body." She pressed a key into his hand. "Here, take this. The house in Riverton wasn't a secret. I could have gone and looked at it myself any time I wanted to."

"Good," Trevor said, and then he waited.

"I want you to take a look to see what he was fixing. He was always handy with tools. And when was the last time you had to ask permission to make your own property a better place?"

Trevor gripped the key. "I'll give it a look," he said.

"Right now. It's a long day tomorrow. You can tell me what you see there. We'll have plenty of time after." She began to whimper, little gasps that lifted into whistling that reminded Trevor of how his mother had sounded when he'd come out to her the day after graduation.

He'd waited through hours with her and his relatives, saying thank-you for each card that had a check tucked inside. He'd waited until two ancient great-aunts left before he'd taken off for a house where a classmate's parents kept an open bar and let them play their stereo at full blast until they fell asleep on couches or the carpet with pillows they found scattered on furniture. He'd even waited through dinner the following night before getting the words out. "Why?" his mother had said just before her shoulders began to heave. "What did I do?" she'd added, before her voice shifted into those gasps and whistles.

By that time Travis had known for three years. "It's how he's wired," he'd said, but his mother had shuddered the way she did when she had to handle what she called the "awful giblets" before she put the Thanksgiving turkey in the oven. "You and your damn sensibilities," he'd shouted when she got up from the table and walked away.

She'd turned at her bedroom door and stared at Trevor. "You've never done that in this house, have you?" she said.

"Done what?" he'd yelled, standing, and she'd slammed the door behind her. They'd never spoke of it again, not even, five years later, when she was dying from the breast cancer she'd kept secret from the doctor for too long.

THE CRIME SCENE TAPE TREVOR HAD SEEN two days ago was gone. The police, he imagined, had decided anything inside was irrelevant or else they were already bored. There was a television set on a hard-backed chair, one other chair just like it, a card table, a table lamp, and a small refrigerator. It looked like what might be found in an adult tree house. Nothing appeared to be restored. Though water ran from the bathroom tap and the toilet flushed, there wasn't furniture in any of the other rooms.

The tv came immediately to life, but without cable there were only three stations with an image, and all of those were obscured by heavy snow. Nobody but the tortured would watch the screen for more than a few seconds, so Trevor knew his brother had used the set for movies, porn maybe, though there weren't any discs in the house that he could see, so maybe Travis had watched *Citizen Kane*. He could ask at the police station, see if they'd taken anything like that as evidence. See if they had a curiosity about just how and why he was poking around inside. In eight days, he thought, the month will end, and soon after or maybe even that very day, this house will go dark. Already, it had the look of a place that would be razed.

He shut the tv off, sat down and bowed his head in the dim light that seeped in from the street. He didn't want a neighbor calling the police. He'd expected to be sad or angry, but now he felt solemn. Like he was already in church. Like looking at his shoes meant he was asking for mercy.

Late on the night of his 30th birthday party, Travis had drunkenly told him, "It's so hard with women. Here I am thirty and what have I ever done? It has to be easier being gay. You know what men want, and there's none of that song and dance that goes with trying to get laid."

"I've never done hookups," Trevor had said. "I've been with Neal since freshman year in college. Ten years. It's different, but the same."

Travis had shaken his head. "You have no idea how hard it is to get a girl into bed." Six months later Travis had married Dakota. At the wedding, Trevor was certain both of them were virgins.

IN THE MORNING TREVOR CARRIED HIS LAPTOP to Starbuck's, a place he was sure would have WiFi. He sipped on coffee at a corner table and logged on to Craig's List, the personals for Williamsport, the closest town on the list of Pennsylvania cities.

Men for Women had nothing but the expected: "Looking for Ms. Right. Married looking for young girl." *Women for Men* had items like "Tired of being lonely" and "Love like you've never been hurt."

Men for Men had twelve messages for the day already: "Looking to suck now. Younger into older play at my hotel." Trevor opened an account and answered three of the messages, promising in each reply that he was submissive and wanted to please.

He ordered a blueberry muffin and another coffee. He read the newspaper's account of the stabber's previous life, her mother's assertion it was devil worship that drove her to kill, an initiation she had been forced into. A picture of the girl as a child was placed alongside the article.

When nearly an hour had passed, he checked back at Craig's List and found a return message from a man who agreed to meet him early the next morning at the overlook at the nearby county park, describing the make and model and color of his car and exactly where it would be parked. The end of the message read, "I want you exposed and on your knees."

After he said "yes," Trevor drove back to the motel, took a long shower, and dressed for the funeral.

THE VIEWING AT THE FUNERAL HOME was packed, but only three cars followed the hearse to the cemetery, so Trevor was surprised to see a minister already at the gravesite. "A price has been paid," the minister began, and Trevor tensed, but the rest was about forgiveness—a loving husband and a man who'd held a steady job and treated others well, a menu of small, good qualities that added up to enough to qualify for a room in heaven.

This minister, Trevor knew, would pronounce him damned because he was guilty, many times over, of an unforgivable sin. He and Travis had laughed about it a few times when Travis admitted he still went to the same church their mother had dragged them to. "Hell won't be so bad," Trevor had said. "It will be full of faggots." It was easy to joke about something Trevor was sure never would happen.

The minister shifted into what seemed to be a standard homily about faith and eternity and belief in the forgiving side of God. "That God," the minister proclaimed, "will accept Travis into his arms."

A child's vision, Trevor thought, and drifted into memory of the toy box their grandfather had made for Travis when he was two, just before Trevor was born. It had always been there in their room, large and painted white with bright red and blue circles, triangles and squares. Bigger than a footlocker, his mother always said, though he hadn't known what a footlocker was until he was ten, and Travis didn't bother with the toy box anymore.

And neither did he after he turned twelve, though one afternoon, when he was thirteen, he'd opened it for the first time in over a year and lifted a few old board games out, laughing at how easy the questions were on the games that said, "for all ages" as if their mother might actually be willing to play. "That thing looks like a coffin big enough to cram your father into if anybody knew where in hell he was ruining somebody's life these days," his mother had said for the past two years. "It needs to go, and so does all that stuff for little boys that neither of you will ever touch again."

It had been Travis who said he liked it sitting there, that it made a shelf for things and maybe he'd like to pass along those old toys to his own sons when he had them. "How about you?" his mother said, and Trevor had agreed that he liked it too.

She'd thrown her hands up. "You're too young to be lost in the past."

But that day, when he'd lifted out a couple of puzzles with large thick pieces that were stuffed under the board games, he found magazines and videotapes and knew why Travis wanted that toy box to stay. He'd slid a video into the VCR, and it began in the middle of a scene with two naked women and a naked man. His eyes had gone immediately to the man's body, and before the scene had ended he'd opened his pants and stroked himself off. He rewound the tape to where it had begun and made sure he put everything back where he'd found it.

He was so careful that it had taken Travis a few weeks before he said, "It's ok, just don't ever forget to put all the toys back. Thirteen, little brother. I know what that's like."

"I hardly ever open it," he'd said, but Travis had cut him off.

"You don't have to lie. Jesus Christ, at first I thought Mom was rooting through the toys. I was picturing her watching half an hour of blowjobs."

After the minister finally shut up and he and Dakota had each tossed a shovel full of dirt onto the casket, Trevor started directly for the hearse, but he paused when he saw that Dakota had stopped to talk with the minister. A moment later, Sandy and her broad-shouldered son, who looked still to be a teenager in jeans and a ball cap, stood beside him as if she was a family member. "Those two fucks will get the needle," she said, but it sounded like she was offering something she'd heard on premium cable television

"No, they won't," Trevor said, but he kept his eyes on the boy.

Sandy glanced to where Dakota still stood with the minister, and then, lowering her voices, she said, "I know he's your brother and all, but Travis deserved being locked the fuck out of Dakota's house long ago, and then maybe all of this wouldn't have happened."

"Shut the fuck up," Trevor said, tensing, his fists balled, but when Sandy hissed once and veered away, her son fell in behind her.

A HALF HOUR LATER, TREVOR SAT WITH DAKOTA in Applebee's with an appetizer sampler of deep-fried finger food. Dakota finished two wings and a mozzarella stick before she spoke. "A whole page of the newspaper was about that bitch this morning. On the day of the funeral, no less. Mark my words, next we'll be seeing her face on the tv."

"Let's hope not," Trevor said, going slow with the grease and fat, but ready to order a second beer.

"Hope is for the religious," she said. "Those two need hell right here and now so we're sure they get what they deserve."

"There's never enough misery to satisfy."

"You notice the newspaper people at the viewing? They left right away after their pictures and such, and you can bet that's the last the world will see of me and Travis."

"Being left alone might be a good thing," Trevor said.

"Don't you bet on that," Dakota said. "I've had plenty of alone." She wiped her hands on a napkin before she picked up her beer mug and drank. "You know what else? Travis was the first man who ever touched me, and now look at me."

"I've only lived with one man that way," Trevor said. "I met Neal in college, and we stayed with each other for sixteen years."

"Safety first, right? But you, if you give it half a try, won't have trouble finding another man, so fit and trim like you are."

"There's more to it than fitness."

"Well, there's Sandy let go of herself years ago and almost forty, but she has men over there all the time. I couldn't do that, could you?"

"No."

"So here we are. Travis had his ways, but he was here, you know?"

"Yes."

"Well then," she said, and Trevor thought of saying "yes" to that as well but let silence settle instead.

THE NEXT MORNING AT 8:15 there were two cars parked together near where the road leveled off into the recreation area that had a few picnic tables, bathrooms; he remembered that the overlook had a fence here because of how many children or careless drunks crowded the edge. It was early, a time when those families and drinkers wouldn't be wandering the park. Trevor was glad for the arrangement. He wasn't climbing into a van where a second man or even a third might be waiting. He wasn't coming here after dark when anything might happen to someone cruising. The man had labeled himself as "mature."

The car the man had described was parked by itself near the rest rooms. No one was inside, but Trevor knew the man must be nearby watching him, evaluating. When he took a few steps toward the densest section of the woods, a figure stepped into view and turned into a narrow path. Like Trevor, the man wore sweatpants and a t-shirt—he looked to be in his fifties, graying, a bit soft in the middle.

Trevor followed. He felt his pulse quicken, the combination of anticipation and fear he hadn't felt since the first semester of college when he hadn't yet come out, not touching another body until he met Neal after the holiday break, and even then, holding back for weeks to be sure he wasn't making a mistake. By the time he reached the spot where the man had stepped off the path, the man's sweatpants were at his ankles. He wasn't wearing underwear. The man, Trevor noticed, wore a wedding ring, and he stared at him until Trevor let his own sweatpants drop. And then his boxers, and both of them stiffened as if being exposed outdoors was as erotic as the touch of hands and lips.

The man was thick and burly, his penis circumcised. Anything could happen now, Trevor told himself as he knelt.

Though he didn't believe that, not even undressed with a stranger, not even when the man pushed into his mouth and gripped Trevor's shoulders hard, using his hands like a weapon.

Real Talking

WHEN KRISTY CHECKED IN WITH THE RECEPTIONIST, she found out her gynecologist had left the practice since her last appointment. "Her replacement is Dr. Mentata," the receptionist said, "but you could see one of the other doctors if you'd like."

"That's ok," Kristy said. "I'm sure she's fine."

The receptionist hesitated. "Dr. Mentata is bilingual," she said.

Kristy had told this story half a dozen times while Gilchrist was nearby, and he laughed every time when she got to "bilingual." Kristy never laughed. She was serious about letting everybody know what a bigoted, ignorant fool the receptionist was. "She wanted me to know the new doctor was Mexican to warn me in case I didn't want 'a foreign.' Bilingual. I understood what she meant, the stupid moron."

The first time he heard the story, Gilchrist suggested that maybe the other doctors had told the receptionist to inform the patients, but Kristy scoffed. "They couldn't have said that," she declared. "No way in hell. They're educated."

Gilchrist had been living with Kristy for nearly two years by then, and it looked as if they might stay together for a good long stretch, both of them close to fifty and maybe ready to finally settle for what they had. Her husband was dead ten years, and she had children grown and gone; Gilchrist had two marriages over and done with, no children he knew of.

She seemed so normal, Gilchrist had thought, what gave him hope that his life might go on unchanged for years. The only odd thing he'd learned about Kristy was the way she carried a rock in her purse everywhere she went. A rock wrapped inside a knotted, double stocking. A weapon. It made her feel better, she'd explained, to have it handy to bash some mugger's head.

Whatever gives you comfort, Gilchrist had thought, but carrying that homemade weapon wasn't the odd part. The weirdness was that the stone had started out as a "pet rock" back when that fad had swept the country for a year. "Really," Kristy had said. "My father gave it to me for my high school graduation. He thought it was the funniest thing because for a few seconds I believed that was all I was getting, a big joke for all those years putting up with school."

Gilchrist had nodded at that. Big jokes weren't up his alley either. Neither was change, not at forty-nine, but Kristy had just entered menopause. She'd scheduled that appointment with the gynecologist because of it, making sure it was something that had happened for ordinary reasons. And for a while he thought it was the menopause, not the prejudice, that had Kristy going. That afternoon she'd swung her old, wrapped up, pet rock from her hand like a pendulum and said, "Maybe I don't need this now. Men don't look at me. They don't think their thoughts."

"Yes, they do," Gilchrist said, wanting to cheer her up.

"Don't you lie to me like I'm an old woman."

"Some do. For sure."

Her expression flickered toward hope and then it went dark. "Yes," she said, "the ones who are awful. The ones who look because they never do."

More than them, Gilchrist wanted to say, but her answer made him think of men who fantasized violence, imagining her a victim. People need to be busy, he thought. Without work we think our worst thoughts, and then some of us act on them.

"Let's fix something," he said instead. "Let's start making this house good as new. You can pick out something snazzy for the kitchen."

"You can't fix anything."

"I can hire somebody. That's what I can do."

TWO WEEKS LATER A WOMAN on their street was raped inside her house in the middle of the afternoon. "Somebody from our street," Kristy said when she heard. "Never in my life have I lived that close to this."

"Once in a lifetime," Gilchrist said. "Like lightning or something."

Kristy flashed him a look that shut him up. "She left her door open while she worked in the yard. He was waiting inside for her." Gilchrist didn't know what to say. "Where are we now?" she said, sounding like she was alone and frightened and talking out loud to herself.

"Those things don't happen in our neighborhood," Gilchrist's mother had said when, as a boy, he'd read about a girl snatched a block from her house in another part of town or a boy beaten by assailants and fighting for his life in the hospital. "That's why your father works so hard, so we can live where all of us are safe."

They'd moved when he was seven and his sister was nine. "It's like heaven here," his mother would say, as if they'd ascended to another life, and he remembered he and his sister, until the day before they'd moved, being told never to leave the yard they had shared with the family who rented the other side of the house. They'd listened. Neither of them had ever wandered off, and neither had ever gone outside without the other. By the time he was eight, he knew that "these things" happened in a neighborhood like the one they'd moved away from.

And they never had, not that he knew of, not even after he realized how absurd his mother's assumptions were. None of the children he knew disappeared. Nobody was robbed or assaulted. Or raped, he thought now, though to think that the parallel streets of twenty houses each that was their neighborhood were free of trouble was a crazy thing to believe. Their street was Reveille Road; above them was Lullaby Lane, some developer once upon a time thinking clever names that suggested, in English, a magical way of life, would attract buyers.

Those streets had become ones where no one had trick-or-treated either October he'd lived there. Dirge Alley, Gilchrist called their street when Halloween past a second time with the candy untouched.

"We're not even fifty," Kristy had said, as if that made the name inaccurate.

"And by the looks of it, we're the youngest," Gilchrist had said.

"It will flip," she'd said. "Give it time."

And what Gilchrist had said then, regretting it now, was, "Until then it's a street where people can't defend themselves."

KRISTY ASKED HIM TO LOCK UP ALL THE TIME. "Promise me," she said, and Gilchrist promised, easy enough, but the nuisance was that she started locking both the screen and the door so he had to ring the bell or knock every time he came home and she was there. And it took her nearly a minute, sometimes more, to answer.

"What takes you so long?"

"I have to go upstairs to see the porch."

He stood in the aging kitchen, looking down at the worn spots in the linoleum. Kristy had lived in this house when Gilchrist still had a second marriage to begin. "You know it's me this time of day," he said, imagining he could settle her down, see to it that she wasn't unhappy.

"And so does he," Kristy said. "I know who he's looking for. Somebody who's not on guard. Somebody who thinks all this is behind her and opens the door like nobody could be there but the man she expects every day."

He knew what she meant by that. The rape victim was nearly sixty years old. When Gilchrist saw her at her mailbox or getting into her car, he took in how trim she looked, like someone who had never had children or a bad habit. Kristy looked like that. Thin. Fit. It made you look younger to a stranger. Or someone he despised.

Gilchrist saw dozens of women who looked like that every day because of his job in a department store. He was the manager of women's clothing, surrounded entirely by women. He felt like a rapist himself, evaluating middle-aged women, ones close enough to his age to not see him as old, ones who were slim-hipped. Louise Craig, for example. Or Carol Sherk. He noticed them because they dressed well for the job. Like he did, a suit every day.

Since he'd taken this position, Gilchrist had always begun his job interviews by assessing the women's bodies. *Wouldn't any man?* he told himself now, hearing the words in his head as if he'd been asked to defend that practice.

He'd turned down some lookers. He could say that, for sure. It was more a question of discouraging those that put him off by being heavy. What he didn't need were women who reminded customers of the hopelessness of new clothes, how they made no difference on bodies gone to seed.

And the women who looked to being quick to judgment. It wasn't all about shape. He couldn't have saleswomen who carried expressions of condemnation, who made customers see themselves more clearly as vain. He was as fair as he could imagine a man being. But Kristy getting spooked like she was turned Gilchrist nervous on the job. He kept busy.

He helped arrange displays. He walked the floor, greeting customers. He wanted to be among his staff, not spending half the day with orders and shipping issues and schedules where his mind wandered, knowing Kristy had herself locked up inside the house.

"THE RAPIST'S FACE WAS COVERED," the victim who lived on their street said in the newspaper article about the crime, "but I heard him speaking Spanish. Whatever he said sounded worse because I couldn't understand it."

Bilingual, Gilchrist thought, but he kept that to himself until Kristy said, "That Goddamned receptionist. All I can think about is her now."

"She must be wrong," Gilchrist said.

"Who? The victim?" Kristy's voice carried a sharpness one pitch below shrill.

"A Hispanic man would be remembered here. He wouldn't attack a woman in a neighborhood like ours. He'd be a sore thumb."

Kristy shook her head. "People would think they knew him until they put him in a lineup with more Hispanics," she said. "And then he'd look like all the rest."

"That can't be true in this day and age."

"Just because people know better doesn't mean they've changed." She rustled the newspaper as she picked it up. "Listen to this," she said, reading aloud: "'No, I don't speak Spanish,' the rape victim admitted, 'but I know it when I hear it.'"

She dropped the paper as if she'd felt some soggy bit of breakfast stuck to it. "What if a man said Spanish words while he was doing it?" she said. "You know—to throw people off."

"Like a disguise?"

"Exactly."

"He'd sound phony. He wouldn't have the right accent."

Kristy glanced back at the newspaper as if support for her argument was printed there. "Just a few words," she said. "He could learn to say them right. He's not reciting the Gettysburg Address."

WHILE HE WAS WANDERING through the department the following day, Gilchrist paused two aisles away to watch Louise Craig working with a customer. "What do you call this, Louise?" the customer asked her, reading her name from the tag pinned to Louise's blouse.

Louise hesitated. "It's a heavy material, isn't it?" she said. "I think it's crocheted."

Gilchrist moved closer as the woman rubbed her fingertips over the material. "Boucle," he said, and Louise's lips tightened.

"Really?" the customer, a woman Gilchrist guessed was in her 50s said, "or are you just saying that?"

"Really."

"Is that a foreign word?"

"Yes," he said, but he could tell she was already retreating, put off by the exotic-sounding name. In a few seconds she was gone. He touched the material for himself as Louise frowned. "This looks like it will snag," he said. "The weave feels slack."

"I know what it feels like to me," Louise said. "It feels heavy. Like armor more than like a vest kind of thing." She pushed at it with her right hand as if she expected to produce a slapping sound, and then she glanced at the next rack. "That dress is ruched," she said. "I know that for a fact."

He touched the ruffle of lace near the collar of one of the dresses on the rack. He could have just nodded, but laying his hand on the lace gave him satisfaction. "And this capelet here," Louise went on, "is designed to slim whoever wears it." She paused. "Jeff," she said, "don't you wish you worked in men's?"

"No," he said at once.

"Oh, you can be honest with me. You'd have somebody to talk to there."

"We're talking," he said. "I talk with all of you."

"You know what I mean. Real talking."

"What's that?" he said, though he understood immediately what she meant and knew that she was right.

"Jeff," she said, "don't pretend now for my sake."

"It's not a problem," he said, forcing himself not to add "really" or "that's God's truth," something like putting an exclamation point at the end to show he meant it because he hadn't done any real talking with anyone for years.

He carried the phrase home with him, intending to start a conversation with Kristy, one that would lead both of them to reveal secrets and wishes. He was so excited he forgot about the locked screen door, yanking the handle and taking the jolt of resistance up his arm into his shoulder. He knocked and peered through the screen, but Kristy wasn't in the kitchen, and he didn't see her emerging from the living room or bedroom. He knocked again, stepping back from the door and glancing up where she might be standing in the window to see.

He rapped harder, and to his surprise, Kristy walked from the living room into the kitchen. "What were you doing?" he started, but she seemed frightened.

"See there?" she said. "I can be so careless. I never thought I would ever just leave the real door open like that."

"It's all right. It was just me."

"Why didn't you say something?"

"I thought you were upstairs." Gilchrist glanced around the kitchen, trying to fix on something ordinary to keep himself grounded.

"I saw a face close to the screen like it was looking right at me, but I couldn't tell who it was. If you had said something, I would have come right away."

"You waited until I started pounding."

"Then I knew it was you."

He turned just enough to look at the refrigerator, where three pictures were held up by magnets—he and Kristy from a year ago, Kristy's children from the Christmas before when they'd visited, and a brand-new photo of her first grandchild.

"I need to work off some steam," he said, tugging his tie down and undoing the knot. "I'll do some yard work with you."

He changed clothes quickly, eager to get outside, but he could hear Kristy checking all three doors. "Do you have your keys?" she said.

"This is crazy. I'm practically going to be right beside you."

"What if you wander off? What if Bob Richardson calls you over for a beer like he does every chance he gets, and you forget about me while you watch baseball?"

"Jesus Christ."

Kristy lifted his keys from the kitchen table and pushed them into his right hand. "You don't have empathy," she said. "I thought it just came and went in you, but now I know it's never there."

"I'm concerned. I'm worried." The words sounded false. They sounded like the phrases of a politician working a blighted neighborhood.

"For yourself," she said. "If I fall apart, it's a problem for you."

"That can't be true," he said, but he went quiet with resignation.

"Whether it is or not, you take your keys with you because I'm locking up."

He opened the refrigerator with his free hand and pulled out a can of beer, snapping it open. "I'll have my beer by myself," he said. "I'll sit inside and keep watch."

"You don't understand," she said. "Somebody was at the door today."

"People do that. There's reasons."

"He drove up in a repair truck of all things."

Gilchrist slapped the keys back down on the table. "Of course he did. I hired him as a surprise," he said. "I wanted you to be excited that you'd have a new floor and new cabinets. Didn't his truck have a sign on it or something that reminded you about my new kitchen promise?" Through the doorway he noticed the stockings with the rock inside lying on the stairs, and he imagined Kristy creeping half way down, the weapon in her hand.

"'Home Repairs and Remodeling,' it said on the driver's side door. It scared me to see that, a man getting out of a truck like that so anybody watching wouldn't think anything about his entering a house."

Seeing that stocking-wrapped rock tightened Gilchrist's chest enough to make him reach through the railing and pull it down. "Leave it alone," Kristy said, but he carried it into the kitchen, which suddenly looked decrepit. Gilchrist imagined how it would look in five years, or ten, the worn spots become holes so you would be able to see the dismal, cheap wood underneath. By then a cupboard or two might be unhinged and drooping, the counter by the sink an accumulation of irremovable stains.

Gilchrist hefted the pet rock. Swung it by the knotted end of the stocking until he thought of David and Goliath. Without an interventionist God, she would be slaughtered.

"You can't hurt anybody with this rock, even swinging it inside these stockings," he said.

"It's not impossible."

"Ok. It's not impossible."

"It's like all the countries that have nuclear bombs. They can't hurt anybody with them. All they can do is have them."

"Deterrence."

"Yes."

Gilchrist let it go. Kristy seemed to be settling. There was no point in saying it was more like a little dog snapping at the ankles of her attacker. It would snarl and nip until it was flung against a wall like a snowball.

He started to think about how long it might take for Kristy to put things in perspective and begin to act like a normal person again. The answer that occurred to him was measured in months, and immediately after, in years. Surely she knew that happiness, even a vague, muted kind, depended on being able to put the inevitable unpleasantness of the world out of your mind. Surely he wouldn't have to say out loud that upset whatever balance he'd acquired for himself?

"That rapist is like the flu," Kristy said at last, her hand on the door knob. "Somebody always gets it no matter what shot the doctors gives us." He nodded, but that, he thought, didn't mean you started wearing a surgical mask like a crazy person.

When she disappeared into the yard, Gilchrist knelt down to examine the spot most worn on the floor. Sure enough, there was a small tear, and he could just make out the dark wood underneath. Later that night, when Kristy was asleep, he remembered his intention to have a real talk with her.

A HALF MILE FROM THEIR HOUSE, just off Washington Street, there was a one-street housing plan that had become a Mexican neighborhood. The road was an all-day sucker shape, straight running into a circle where, Gilchrist thought, English was a second language by design. The town had changed the name of the street from Creek Road to Los Angeles Way twenty years back when what the old-timers still called "the influx" had arrived. The town council said the change was out of respect, that they meant it as welcoming, but all the while they were solidifying a segregation plan with that name, substituting acknowledgement for acceptance. Just half a mile away and yet neither Gilchrist nor Kristy had ever driven up that street, but one Sunday, coming home from buying groceries together, Gilchrist believed it would do Kristy some good for him to turn left on Los Angeles Way.

Something like getting back behind the wheel after you'd been in an accident. Something easy because it wasn't even your accident to recover from. Something necessary because you can't let yourself be changed by somebody else's problem or pretty soon you'd end up helpless.

Gilchrist drove slowly. Kristy looked at him like he was a dog tugging his leash toward wet, snarled underbrush. "Relax," Gilchrist said. "It's just one loop around and out again."

He held out his right hand, but Kristy didn't take it. She crossed her arms under her breasts and stared straight ahead as they passed houses small enough that Gilchrist remembered the word *bungalow*. With the window down, he could smell barbecue. *Cumin*, he thought. *Cilantro*. He loved those spices, but they smelled foreign outside, unlike any of the dark red barbecue sauces he kept in the refrigerator for early evening cookouts. Two men in sleeveless undershirts looked up from a side yard grill, staring.

"You're thinking they're all bilingual, aren't you?" Kristy said, not smiling.

"And they all think we're not," he said, realizing, when she refused to turn her head, his tough-love experiment was already collapsing.

Gilchrist noticed three young men sitting on the stone steps leading up to a front porch. Kristy held her pose as they passed, but none of the young men eyed the car for more than a few seconds. *They would show the same interest in a squirrel*, Gilchrist thought. "Your doctor doesn't live here," he said. "She doesn't live where we do either."

"You never even saw her."

"I don't have to."

"I wish I hadn't told you that story. It brings out something ugly in you."

They finished the loop, catching just one brief bit of Salsa music being played to an empty yard. Back on Washington, they passed nothing but white people. It wasn't any different than traffic on their street, but Kristy went quiet, considering him. "There's never anybody bilingual in my department either," he said, and she faced forward, drifting so close to the edge of the sidewalk there was room for a third person between them. *Like Jesus*, Gilchrist thought, *that time he walked stride for stride to Emmaus with two men after he'd risen from the dead in that Bible story.*

He fought down the temptation to say it aloud. He didn't need to add disgust to her list of feelings for him. He wanted to tell Kristy that story and knew she'd be horrified and disgusted, but he didn't need to condemn himself.

AT WORK THE NEXT AFTERNOON he walked among racks of Liz Claiborne, Emma James, ellen tracy, and Rafaella. In the center of those familiar names was a rack of Chaus dresses, a smaller selection, more expensive than their customers were usually willing to pay. From there he listened to three of the saleswomen—Louise and Carol and Arlene Czak--talk among themselves. They spoke in a tone that only women seemed to use. *What was it?* he thought, and words like *soft* and *feminine* came unsatisfactorily to mind. *Solicitous*, he thought. It sprang up like a perfect, timely answer, and Gilchrist repeated it until it sounded as wrong as the simpler words.

He knew they had an alternate tone as well, one that his mother used to call "catty." "You know what she's been up to," he would overhear. "Did you see how she was dressed?" But when one of them had a problem, the tone reversed to solicitous.

When he drifted past them, they quieted, looking away until he reached the end of the department where a large stand of North American Stitchery items were displayed, the house brand, all of it made in Mexico.

THE NEWSPAPER BEGAN RUNNING a series of articles on violence toward women. Domestic abuse, for one. How rapists were turned on by power, not sex, for another. Experts were interviewed, and among the quotes from rape victims in the area were more from the neighborhood victim. "He was so young," she said. "That's what surprised me. Not that he spoke Spanish. I could see his age around his eyes. Nobody over thirty looks like that. You know—smooth like he's just out of high school or something, like he's almost a boy. There's no way an ordinary boy his age would be interested in somebody like me."

"See?" Kristy said.

"What's that mean?" Gilchrist said, because he couldn't see how the rapist's age changed anything.

"I guess you can't feel what it's like."

He wanted to argue now, but Gilchrist stayed quiet. They'd fought before, but it wasn't her anger he was worried about. It was her fear, that whatever he said next would terrify her.

"A young man," she said. "A boy. You can't imagine how that makes me feel."

"I guess not," Gilchrist said. She stood and moved behind him, laying her hands on his shoulders. For a moment, he thought it was over, and he turned in his chair, but she dropped her hands and took a step back. "I'm going to bed early," she said. "This business has me worn out."

"You remember sand-breeding?" Gilchrist said, calling after her as she walked into the bedroom.

When she reappeared, holding her night gown, Gilchrist grew hopeful. "No," she said, and he spoke quickly.

"It's what the pet rock guy tried next, but nobody remembers anymore because that idea flopped."

Kristy stepped into the doorway to the bathroom. "I moved out," she said. "I wasn't around to have my father give me a pile of sand for my nineteenth birthday."

She closed the bathroom door behind her. A few minutes later she came out dressed for bed, turning off the bedroom light as she passed the switch by the door.

"WHAT'S THIS ALL ABOUT?" Gilchrist said the third night she undressed for bed in the bathroom.

Kristy turned off the light before she dropped her blouse and her underwear in the hamper. He heard her fumbling in the closet and knew she was hanging up her skirt. She'd heard him. He wasn't going to ask a second time. When she lay down on the bed, he flipped the switch on his reading light, sat up, and looked at her. "People can see," she said.

"What people? Our neighbors across the street?"

"Whoever's out there."

"Nobody's ever out there. The street's empty. Nobody has kids around anymore. We might be the youngest people on the street."

"You sound like you've been waiting to say all that. You sound creepy the way you say it."

He looked at the drawn blinds and back at Kristy. "You already have those things to keep people from seeing."

"Have you ever gone outside and checked to see if they work?"

"You know what's creepy, don't you? Listen to yourself."

She turned away from him, pulling the sheet up to her chin. He watched her breathing for a minute before he turned off the light. Touching her was out of the question. After another week of it, he rolled over and closed his eyes before she finished in the bathroom. He waited for her to say something, but when she got into bed it was like he wasn't there.

HE WAS UPSTAIRS READING when someone rang the bell at the front door. He stayed in the low-slung, soft chair while Kristy plodded up the steps and peered out the hallway window. "Damn," he heard her whisper, and she hurried back down, opening the door. He heard a man's voice, and when the door stayed open for a minute before it closed again, he glanced outside and saw it was the mailman.

"I guess you had to sign," he said from the balcony. "If it had taken you a few more seconds, you could have ended up going to the post office for it."

"I had to look. Who knows who it is until they look? And anyway, if I'm so slow, you could have just answered."

He leaned over the balcony and stared at her without speaking. "What?" she said, "are you making a study of me?"

"It's called eye contact."

"It's called spying. Like doctors do. Or like the police."

"Jesus, Kristy."

"That's what it is—a stakeout." She walked to the window and looked outside at the street, her back to him. "They'll catch this guy, won't they? They're watching for him, aren't they?"

"Sure."

"And then things will go back to the way they were."

"Let's hope."

She whirled around. "It's not about hope. I said they will, and that's what I meant."

Let's hope formed a second time behind his lips, but he choked it back. "Good," he said.

"It won't be long. A guy like that takes chances and gets caught."

"And the Spanish thing sets him apart."

"That's not what sets him apart," she said. "You know that as well as I do."

"We should have somebody over," Gilchrist said. "The yard looks so good we should show it off."

"It doesn't need to be seen," Kristy said. "And anyway, I don't want so many people around. Don't you feel like that sometimes? Like you wanted fewer people in the day you were living through?"

"I feel like that most days," he said, but her expression stayed fixed in neutral as if his answer had changed nothing.

WHEN GILCHRIST WALKED THE AISLES the next afternoon, he let his fingertips run over the material of items he passed. Silk, cotton, all of the hybrids. He could go blind and be a salesman, he thought. He could listen to a woman and know what she wanted from these clothes. He lifted the sweater—From Wine to Riches it said on the label. He flipped the turtleneck collar forward and reversed the arms, folding the sweater back before they could slide and dangle. During training, a saleswoman had taught him the technique, watching him until he could manage. He'd asked her if she worked in the store, and she'd said "No," not smiling.

"Purple Swirl" it said on the label of the sweater next to From Wine to Riches. He refolded it so tight it looked as if it were pinned together.

A moment later, when he walked into the storage room, he saw Carol Sherk. She was hunting for something, absorbed, and for a moment she didn't seem to sense that he was there. She was kneeling, looking along a low shelf, her skirt pulled tight over her hips, and he closed the door behind him to let her know he was there.

She stood up so quickly, half-turning, that she nearly lost her balance. "Oh God, Jeff," she said, "you scared me there for a second."

"Sorry," he said, but Carol looked past him at the closed door.

"I'll come back later," she said. "It's not that big a deal."

"Ok," he said, but she didn't move, and he understood she was waiting for him to step aside.

Gilchrist shuffled to his left between two rows of shelves before Carol moved, walking quickly, and he knew that if he stepped toward her she would scream. Another second and she was gone, leaving the door wide open.

EARLY THE NEXT AFTERNOON, a Thursday, when nearly every husband was away at work, Gilchrist unlocked the side door while Kristy was in the yard. His day off. But he wore a suit and didn't close the door behind him, so anyone could see it was open. He drove away, looped back after a quarter mile, and parked on Lullaby. If the rapist was watching the house, he would move in now.

He could see Kristy in the yard, and he kept his eyes on the side door, waiting. For half an hour, nobody approached the house. This was a way to save Kristy, he had told himself, but his scheme, by now, seemed as improbable as faith healing, and the anticipation drained out of him like the sweat that stuck his shirt to his back and chest.

It would be easier to examine a woman you didn't know, he thought. To stalk her. To see her as nothing but a body. To be a housebreaker.

Gilchrist wiped the sweat off his forehead with his hand, suddenly sure someone was watching him, a neighbor on Lullaby who didn't recognize him, who believed she was solving a crime while she kept an eye on him and punched in 911.

What would he tell someone who came out of a nearby house to ask what he was doing? That he was sick? That he'd grown sleepy and pulled off the road to rest because of the street name?

He got out of the car and began to walk. It gave him more options for excuses, he thought, though none came to him.

But it was hard to see his house and yard clearly from other angles. They were out of view for brief times as he passed each house. Even as he got back in the car, restoring his clear view, seeing Kristy and the open side door again, he remembered the moments when he couldn't see that door as he walked.

No one approached the car. The police didn't arrive. But after five more minutes, Kristy went to the front door, unlocked it, and as soon as she disappeared inside Gilchrist imagined that the rapist had slipped in so quickly he was already in the house by the time he'd parked the car.

Gilchrist got out of the car and walked into the closest yard. He needed to see better. It had been two minutes, three at most, but what he was imagining was possible. The rapist could be inside with Kristy now.

Such a slim chance, and yet Gilchrist began to run, cutting through two yards, dashing across the road, and scrambling onto the side porch. He pulled at the screen door he'd left open, but it was locked. Kristy had secured it again. *Or someone else had*, he thought, because she would have shut and locked the side door as well.

He pounded on the screen door. "Kristy," he called, his voice cracking, sounding young, and when he heard someone walking, he held his breath, trying to remember the sound of her footsteps, whether these were ones he should know.

"What?" he heard her say from the shadowed hall. "Who is it?" She sounded like someone with a knife pressed against her throat, like someone frightened by the sound of her name. Gilchrist needed to sound like himself. To swallow and clear his throat. To utter the simplest, normal words.

See What I See

In October,1985, a few weeks after I'd started eighth grade, my mother shot my father's lawn six times, her aim sweeping from left to right as if she was drawing a line. "God damn you and this place," she said before each shot, sneering like the girls who helped Patrick Swayze terrorize the Russians who invaded her town in *Red Dawn* when I'd seen it at the Twins, our second-run movie theater.

She was sure my father was inside the house because his car was parked in the driveway, a handy clue because the one-car garage hadn't had room for either my father's Ford or my mother's Nissan Sentra since I could remember because it was full of old lawnmowers and rusted tools, three broken televisions, a washer and dryer set, and an ancient refrigerator my mother had made him take the door off "before your only son suffocates himself in there."

"You cowardly, silent shit," she said when she was finished, pointing the empty gun at each of the four windows in the front. Behind one of them, she must have believed, my father was peeking, and then she climbed into the car where I was sitting with my seat belt on like I'd promised.

"Good boy," she said, patting me on my head. I almost barked, but thought better of it. She stuffed the pistol under her seat and started the car. "I considered shooting holes in all those damned, broken appliances, but I finally decided to shoot the lawn so every neighbor who cared to look could see how Mr. Keeps-to-Himself stayed inside and took it."

I looked at the lawn as if I expected the holes to be bleeding. "He'll have his hands full with the shame," she went on. "He'll have some explaining to do."

I wondered if you could get arrested for assaulting a yard, even one as small and weed-choked as my father's, with dandelions so thick it looked as if they'd been planted as ground cover. "If he presses charges," my mother said like a mind-reader, "your father could complicate things." We were moving by then, back on the busy two-lane that ran six houses down from where we'd lived until two weeks before. She patted my left knee. "But don't you worry. I know your father. This will be the beginning and end of it. It's just one more thing he'll never talk about the rest of his life. He's like those World War II vets who keep everything to themselves, even now when there as old as dirt. D-Day, Iwo Jima, the Battle of the Bulge and all that. Like they ate something terrible and can't digest it." I knew she meant me to remember that her father, who'd died three years ago, had been one of those guys instead of me thinking he'd been outright scary with never talking about anything, let alone what had happened to him almost thirty years before I was born.

"Ok," I said, but she'd already reached for the radio and turned on the NPR station that was playing what sounded like a hundred violins pretending to be an approaching thunderstorm. "We'll stop for pizza," she said. "There's a three-topping special at Gino's. You can get whatever tickles your fancy."

Pepperoni. Sausage. Ham. That's what I ordered. She'd promised and she kept her word just like murdering the grass after my father had called my school three times to tell them I wasn't a resident of the district anymore because he figured us for moving in with my Aunt Jeanne, who lived close but over the county line. Two weeks earlier, she'd told my father as we left with a car full of clothes, "You do anything but leave us alone, you'll be sorry," keeping the topping for that particular pizza to herself.

"It's his gun," she said after I'd stuffed myself, eating the whole medium pie except for one slice my mother nibbled. "I thought he would use it on himself. A month ago, I thought maybe my taking it and hiding it would get him to talk."

"He could have hurt you and made you tell him where."

"Not your father. Never," she said, but there was nothing that sounded like admiration in the way she spoke. She stopped on the bridge my old school bus crossed every morning and afternoon, the one where, sitting up high, you were reminded there was nothing but emptiness between that bus and the river all the way down a hundred feet below. "Help me," she said. "Watch where this goes so you know this happened."

"Ok," I said, but I took a step back from the railing, terrified I'd lean over and somehow flop into the air.

"Scaredy-cat," she said, and when I didn't budge, she just let the gun drop, making sure I couldn't see it fall, and the river was so far away that the sound of the splash didn't reach us. "There," she said, but I thought she was pleased that for all I knew it had grown wings and flown away.

MY MOTHER WAS A REAL ESTATE SALESWOMAN, which had come in handy when she'd taken me and a car full of clothes out the front door at the end of September. We'd needed a place to live, and she had the inside dope on an apartment for rent that was three miles from my father but still inside my school district. Just as important, it was furnished, although it felt like my grandmother's house with all the overstuffed, slipcovered chairs and a television that sat on top of a speaker within a cabinet that closed with a loud click as if it could lock itself.

There was a second floor to the house, but the stairs leading up ended at three where a dry wall had been dropped into place and painted the same pale green as the rest of the living room. The owner's mother had lived there until he'd put her in a nursing home, and he told us he'd lived upstairs for the past seven years, keeping his privacy with that redesign.

My mother paid for cable. "We're angry, Jerry, but we're not poor," she said. Now, though, she turned away from our street and drove a mile to where there was a house she'd just sold. "Wait until you take a look at this, Jerry," she said as she unlocked the front door. "But take your shoes off first."

The kitchen was split by a stove. Above it hung gleaming pots and pans and a set of glistening knives. "It looks like a chef lives here, doesn't it?" my mother said. All the furniture was still in the living room. The couch and two oversized chairs were black leather, the carpet so white I thought no one would ever wear shoes in there. Each wall had framed, black and white charcoal drawings, what looked to be one woman's face showing a variety of expressions. "Sit yourself down here with me," she said. "See what it feels like."

She waited until I sat down before settling close to me. "Your father turned out to be a joyless man," she said.

"What's so bad about that?" I said, and when she reached her hand toward me, I scooted back on the couch so quickly she brought that hand to her hair, brushing away a few strands from her face.

"He kept to himself," she said, and after a pause, "completely." And after another pause, "since you started school."

She was struggling so hard I knew she was talking about sex, and I subtracted the eight years from her age of 35 to make her 27 and alone in a house with a man and a boy. I felt old, like I knew something I shouldn't, like I'd caught her touching herself the way I'd been doing every night for almost two years, unable to sleep unless I felt that spasm that was never anything but incredible.

"You don't have to answer, Jerry," she said. "You're thirteen. I know you understand these things now."

I nodded, but it felt like a reflex, like when a fly or something worse lands on your arm or your face. "You think thirty-five is old, but it's not," she said. "Don't hate me for that."

She brushed her hair back again, looking toward the wall the couch faced where the woman's charcoal-shaded lips were pressed together as if she was afraid to show her teeth. "Come on," she said, "let's take a look upstairs."

There were four bedrooms, but all of the doors were closed. "Let's not disturb anything," she said, going to a window at the end of the hall. "If you look off to the side here, you can get an idea of what you'd see if one of the bedrooms on your left was yours."

When I pressed close to the glass and looked, I could see down into the river valley, a part that was farther upstream than the bridge where my mother had dumped the gun, a part that was so heavily wooded it looked like nobody lived there. "From here you'd never know there was a town anywhere nearby," my mother said from behind me. "It's like you live in the only house for miles."

THAT NIGHT, AS IF MY MOTHER wanted to see whether or not her shooting the lawn had been reported, we watched the news on television together. There was a feature on Christa McAuliffe, the woman who had won the contest to be the first teacher in space. "Just think," my mother started, but then she said, "You have a teacher you wish had been picked to go on that ride?"

"I don't know."

"And not come back?" she said, and I blurted, "Mr. Purcello" and laughed because I thought she wanted me to.

"Who's he? I never heard you even mention him."

"He's the shop teacher."

"I thought shop was where the dumb boys go while you're in algebra and science a year early."

"In eighth grade, everybody takes shop."

"Really? How quaint. Just don't come home and tell me you cut your fingers off."

We watched Christa McAuliffe tumble around in the simulator that made the world have no gravity. She smiled in her space suit. "If they ever have a contest for the first real estate agent in space, I'll send my application in. I'm not that old."

"Everybody would want you to show them a house when you got back," I said.

She smiled. "Maybe they would, Jerry," she said. "Maybe I could sell so many houses we could move into one like where we were a little while ago."

"This one's ok," I said, but she turned off the television and stood up like she expected me to follow.

"I'd take them to an upstairs window and show them the view, and they'd be thinking that their agent had been way up there in space where they'll never be. It would make them appreciate seeing for a few miles. They'd want to stand there and look in the mornings when the day was still waiting to happen."

I DREADED GOING TO SCHOOL THE NEXT MORNING. I'd been in the car during the shooting because we had off school for Columbus Day, a holiday the school used by having open house each year. "I guess we skipped it this year," my mother said. "Anyway, aren't you too old for that?"

What she wasn't worrying about was Sharon Rohr, who was in my home room. Sharon lived across the street from my father. We'd even been friends for a while when we'd played together as little kids, but now she was popular. Not cheerleader popular, but smart and pretty popular. It didn't matter if my father kept quiet if she made sure everybody knew my mother was an outlaw, but by the end of the day I knew she hadn't said a word and there was nothing on the news that night either. My mother seemed glad. "Things can happen," she said, "and then disappear."

On Wednesday Sharon, with another pretty girl named Heather beside her, said, "I'm having a party a week from Saturday, Jerry. Sort of for Halloween, but no costumes. Halloween's not until the middle of the next week anyway, but what I'm saying is you're invited, and you know where I live so I don't have to give you directions, and it starts at eight and goes to eleven."

She talked so fast I knew she was nervous, and Heather nodded like she was adding an exclamation point, but I was sure this was my happiest moment of 1985.

THE DAY OF THE PARTY my mother talked me into taking a shower and getting dressed early for the party by promising we'd go out to the Oasis, my favorite restaurant where I could eat tacos and cheese-slathered nachos that wouldn't splatter all over me if I was careful. "Not like those chicken wings you like or worse, spaghetti," she said. "Those always make a mess." At six o'clock, while my mother was telling me how handsome I looked in a sweater she called "preppy," our doorbell rang, and my mother said "I'll get it." I heard her talking for half a minute before she said, "Jerry, come here and meet somebody."

The visitor was already inside the living room. He was wearing a dark blue blazer and a light blue shirt, but not a tie. He carried more weight around his stomach than my father, but what I kept looking at was his beard, thick and black like he was working with Paul Bunyan. "This is Marvin," my mother said.

"Hey there, junior," Marvin said, and stuck out his hand as if his arm could uncoil and reach across the room to where I'd stopped.

"Hi," I said, but I didn't come any closer.

"Marvin won't bite, Jerry," my mother said. "It turns out he wants to treat us both to that dinner I promised. Aren't we lucky? Here you are all dressed up for the party, and we'll have a nice dinner like you're going to the prom."

At the Oasis, my mother ordered rum and cokes and laughed a lot; Marvin drank Coronas that came with a slice of lime he stuffed down the bottle's throat before he put his thumb over the top and shook. We sat there for over an hour, and Marvin paid with cash, making a big thing out of telling the waiter to keep the change. While we waited near the door, he went to the bar and bought a six pack because my mother, during the meal, had said she didn't keep beer in the house.

He opened a can in the car. "You finish that while I drop off Jerry," my mother said, unlocking the door and putting the beer in the refrigerator before we got in her car for the five-minute drive. When she stopped two houses before Sharon's, I thought she was going to give me an inspection, make sure I hadn't splattered grease on myself, but she said, "This is as far as I go, Jerry. I'll be back sitting right here at eleven o'clock sharp."

Sharon had made a mix tape for the party, ninety minutes of songs she and her friends thought were the best ever like "Every time You Go Away" by Paul Young, which was playing when she started talking to me without any of her friends standing beside her. I was working up the courage to ask her to dance when "Brothers in Arms" began, Mark Knopfler's guitar resonating in a way that made me believe the world was a sad place redeemed only by loyalty. "My favorite song," I said

"I love it too," Sharon said, "but it's really hard to dance to. Let's go upstairs. Nobody will think we're doing anything for two minutes. I want to show you something. We can listen from there."

Her room didn't look like what I thought a girl's room would. She didn't have any stuffed animals on her bed; there wasn't anything pink. But the two walls without windows or closets were covered with posters, one all movies, the other all rock bands. Above her bed were movies I loved like *Firestarter, Buckaroo Bonzai, Streets of Fire,* and *Red Dawn,* but what made me stare were her music posters because they formed a wall of women: Heart. Stevie Nicks. Cyndi Lauper. Kate Bush. Joan Jett.

"Nice lineup," I said, and felt like a fool.

"I wish I had more room," Sharon said. "Isn't it weird how you're not supposed to be in here and yet you used to be all the time way back when I had Sesame Street pictures everywhere?"

"Until first grade."

"Exactly. But I was never in your room."

"Because my father worked nights and he was always sleeping."

"You know I saw everything last week," she said. "Your mom is some kind of bad ass."

"She's usually not like that."

"I bet. What were you doing all that time sitting in the car? I didn't think you could lock somebody inside like in a cell or something."

"She told me to stay there," the truth, but it sounded so sissified I expected her to laugh and leave.

Instead, she reached out and put her hands on my shoulders. "And you did," she said, pressing her lips against mine as if obedience were erotic. My hands clutched at her, but she stepped back and I let go. "Well," she said, and it sounded like something that needed to be translated.

I heard Mr. Mister start singing their big hit "Broken Wing," a song I thought only girls could like. "Take a look," she said. "See what I see." I went to the window and tugged the drapes apart. Across the street my father's house was dark except for the glow of the television in his bedroom. He must have lugged the tv in there after we'd moved out, and somehow that seemed terrible. "I never see your Dad," she said. "I mean it. Never. It's like he's a hermit or something."

"He has a job." She was so close behind me, her breath was on my neck.

"It's like he comes and goes after he makes sure nobody is watching."

I felt like slapping her. I turned, but when my right hand rose, I slipped it behind her head and pushed my lips against hers while my fingers snagged in her hair. "Ow," she said, and I untangled myself while she pressed against me as if that would put slack in the tangles.

"You kids should be downstairs," her mother said, suddenly standing in the doorway.

"We're just remembering stuff."

"The pizzas are on their way."

"Ok," Sharon said, but her mother waited until we started down the stairs before she turned off the light, closed the bedroom door and followed us.

The pizzas were from Gino's, and I had to settle for plain because I waited with Sharon while she was being polite and letting everybody take a slice. We danced to three songs, and I danced once with Heather, who talked the whole time, asking me questions as if she was trying to figure out why Sharon Rohr was interested in an ordinary guy like me. At eleven, everybody spilled outside at the same time, and I moved toward the waiting cars as if my mother's was among them before turning left and heading toward where she waited. "Your father's up late with his television," she said as she turned around in a driveway and let the cars thin out. And then, before I could answer, she said, "Did you have a good time?" like I imagined everyone had been asked in the other cars.

A song called "Dominique" was being talked about on the NPR station as we drove home. "When I was your age I loved this song," my mother said.

"That doesn't sound like it would ever be on a real radio station," I said.

My mother laughed and patted my knee. "But it was, and it was Number One and she was on Ed Sullivan. They called her Sister Smile. When we heard it back when you were still riding in a car seat, your father said the Dominique song was the worst thing that ever happened because it ruined her as a nun. I told him she was better off ruined than being cooped up and kept ignorant by the Pope and that bunch."

"So she quit being a nun?" I said. "I thought you weren't allowed to quit."

My mother swung into the driveway and turned off the car. "Well then, you learn everything there is to learn," she said, "so you know what you're getting into beforehand and nobody can take advantage."

"Marvin's gone?" I said when I didn't see his car parked on the street.

"Saturdays only," my mother said, as if she was on a diet that allowed her to binge one day per week.

"SO," I SAID THE NEXT MORNING, "he's coming back next week?"

"Yes."

"Why him?"

"Look," she said. "I left college to marry your father because I was pregnant with you. I was Catholic then, but now I'm not, and I'm thirty-five and you're about ready to take care of yourself without worrying about what I do for a little happiness."

"What about Dad?"

"What about him? Don't feel sorry for him. Back in that little garage of his, hidden among all that trash, your father kept dozens of movies," she said. "He could have opened a store."

"I never saw him watching any."

My mother laughed bitterly. "You don't get it, do you?"

"I guess not" was all I could think of to say.

"They were the kind of movies I hope you never feel the need to watch. His own private stock. He didn't need me anymore. Now do you get it?"

"Yes," I said, but I didn't, not completely anyway, wanting to ask when he watched and where my mother was and whether she ever looked at one or a dozen other questions I could never ask.

ALL WEEK AT SCHOOL I SAID "HI" TO SHARON, but nothing else because she was always with Heather and two or three other girls. The next Saturday my mother brought two six packs home with her from the grocery store and put them in the refrigerator before lunch. "Dad never drank," I said.

"He was too busy with himself," she said, her tone angry, as if she was sick of hearing me mention him. While I was eating a sandwich, Marvin showed up. "Hey there," he said, but then he looked at my mother as if he wanted to ask her something.

"Jerry's off to see the world from his bike," she said. "There won't be many more perfect days like this one with November beginning."

I announced I'd be back for dinner. "We'll order in pizzas," she said. "At five o'clock, ok? Wear your watch."

Marvin looked at the kitchen clock as if we needed to synchronize our watches, but I didn't worry about killing time because I'd been planning where I was going and what I was going to do all week.

Still, I rode around for half an hour before I found myself at the bridge where my mother had dumped the gun. I inched myself to the rail and made myself lean over to see if there was a ledge where the gun might be lying, but there was nothing between me and the distant river but space, and I pushed back, shaking in spite of myself.

Ten minutes later my father's car wasn't in the driveway when I reached his house, but I rode past two more houses before I pushed my bike behind a row of forsythia bushes and walked back. The garage was unlocked like it had been for years because, my mother always said, "Maybe somebody will come and steal everything in there."

I closed the door behind me just in case my father showed up, and then I started looking everywhere I thought a stack of videotapes might be hidden, even looking inside the refrigerator with no door as if they might be hiding in plain sight like the letter in the Poe story we'd read in English class in September.

I went back over every place again, but there weren't any tapes, and I thought for a moment that my mother had lied, that she wanted to give me a reason to despise my father and figured I could never prove she wasn't telling the truth. I wished I'd brought my old house key. I wished my father was the kind of person who left his house unlocked. And then I pulled the shelves out of the refrigerator and crammed myself inside it, pulling my knees up to my chin and hunching over. The space was so small I couldn't, even as a little boy, have crawled inside unless I'd pulled out a shelf, but sitting there, curled up tight on myself, I understood that my father had moved the tapes into the house after we'd left, that all of them were in his bedroom with the television.

For ten minutes, I sat there as if I wanted my father to come home, open the garage door, and find me, but finally I crawled out and settled for leaving the shelves stacked against the side of the refrigerator. I walked around back and cut across two yards before I dragged my bike from behind the forsythia. I pushed it past my father's house and Sharon's, walking beside it until I climbed on when I reached the highway. I had two hours I would spend at the mall before I pedaled home and found out my mother had ordered two medium pizzas, one of them the meat lover's special. When they arrived, Marvin paid, then waited a few seconds before he folded two one dollar bills and pushed them into the delivery man's jacket pocket while I watched.

MONDAY MORNING, OUTSIDE OF HOME ROOM, Sharon was standing between two girls who were both named Laurel. They looked like bookends, both facing her. Or bodyguards, I thought, but I started to talk while I walked toward her, saying "Sharon," interrupting the Laurels, and spilling out, "Do you want to go to a movie on Saturday?"

The Laurels squinted as if they didn't recognize me, but Sharon smiled and said, "I'd love to."

"We can go to whichever one you want to see at the Twins."

"Ok," she said. "I'll look it up in the paper."

I wanted to tell her about Marvin. I wanted her to hate him too. But the Laurels were standing there examining me, and I walked into home room, satisfied with doing half of what I wanted.

SHARON PICKED *ST. ELMO'S FIRE*, which was playing at the Twins because it had come out in June and was bargain priced before it ended up at the video store. It was R rated like *Red Dawn* had been, but nobody checked at Twins. Her older sister Jennifer drove us and stayed to watch it a second time because Rob Lowe was her favorite actor. She sat three rows in front of us, so, she said, "I won't spoil your fun."

"I could have dropped you off," she said on the way back to Sharon's.

"My mother doesn't mind," I said. I didn't need to tell her I wanted to keep my mother away from Marvin for half an hour, maybe get him to go home early because she wouldn't want him in the house after he'd finished his beer. "I told her 10:30, and it's already 10:15, so it won't be long."

"Maybe she'll be late," Jennifer said. "You can stay outside and hope."

We stood there for a minute, side by side but not touching. "Your Dad's watching tv like he always does," Sharon finally said. "I remember the time he showed your home movies backwards when we were little. My Mom and Dad were there. Jennifer, too. Everybody laughed but your Mom when he ran it backwards and you and her jumped out of the lake you were in some place."

"He did that all the time, even when nobody else was around, so my Mom knew what was coming. She thought it was like watching tv reruns all summer."

"It still seems funny. You and her standing in the water and then shooting up and landing on the dock. Your mother held her nose."

I looked at the flickering light in my father's room for a few seconds and reached for Sharon's hand. For a moment, I held my breath as she let me fold my hand over hers. I hoped my mother would be late. I hoped Marvin would drive away drunk and roll off the bridge and sink beside my father's gun. I gripped her hand tighter and tried to think of something to say. "Let's look for the holes in your yard," she said. "I bet we can dig out the bullets."

She tugged my hand, and I was happy to follow, cutting between the crabapple trees that shaded the front of the yard. The television was flickering in my father's room, but the drapes were pulled shut. "Just be quiet," I said, and we knelt down and started peering the grass and dandelions as if we were looking for a contact lens. I thought I knew where the holes were, but it had been almost three weeks, and even though it was late October and the grass wasn't growing, we didn't find anything.

"This is impossible," she said.

"Almost."

"It's like your yard is Jesus or something. Like it's been crucified."

"You have to stay quiet," I whispered. "My Dad's right there," but she kept talking out loud.

"So why did your parents split up anyway?"

"He was unfaithful," I said, the truth.

"Let's peek in on Daddy," she said. "Maybe we can see what he's doing in there. Maybe he has somebody in there with him."

"He doesn't," I said. "He's not doing anything."

"Nobody does nothing."

"Yes, they do."

She started to get up, and when I grabbed her arm, she tumbled down beside me. I knelt over her, my hands on either side of her head, and she lay there, her breath a small fog. "Well?" she said.

Because she didn't lift her head, I had to lower myself onto her to kiss her, and she didn't lift her arms. She lay there like she was dead, and I felt myself stiffen, her mouth opening and our tongues meeting. A set of headlights swept up the road and stopped, the beams throwing everything into shadows and light. "Wow," Sharon said. "I could feel you," but by then I was pushing up and rocking back so I could stand.

"Is that all it takes to get you like that?" she said, standing up and brushing herself off.

The headlights went off, but it seemed brighter anyway, as if the moon had come out from behind clouds, and I knew it was because my father had turned on the light in his room. I thought my father had been watching us, not knowing who we were, impatient maybe for Sharon to be undressed. Even from the back, I was afraid my father would recognize me, and I gripped Sharon hard and said, "Don't turn around."

I guided her between the crabapple trees, the branches snagging against us before releasing to whip the air behind us. As we crossed the street, my mother stepped out of her car two doors down and gestured.

"Where did you two come from?" my mother said as we walked toward her.

"We went for a walk."

"In the dark and so late?"

'There's lights on all over."

My mother glanced toward the house. "Even your father's. He used to be such an early bird on the weekends." She looked at Sharon as if she was inspecting her. "How was the movie?"

"Fantastic," Sharon said, sounding like somebody I didn't know.

SUNDAY MORNING, I GOT UP just in time to watch the ten a.m. news to work on current events for my social studies assignment. I had a blanket pulled around me because my mother didn't have the heat on, and it had turned cold overnight.

Christa McAuliffe was on again, but nothing seemed new except it looked like January might be the launch date. "That teacher is lucky she's someplace warm," my mother said from behind me, placing her hands on my shoulders in a way that made me pull the blanket tighter. "They never launch those rockets from any place where it snows."

She stayed that way, leaning on me a little as we watched until the feature ended. "They can't get enough of that teacher going to space, can they? It's been years since that shuttle was news, and here it is all the time on television."

"She's almost ready to go," I said, sitting forward so her hands dropped away.

"You think she's pretty?" my mother said, staying behind me.

"I guess."

"She's older than I am. She's 37." I shut off the television, but I didn't say anything else. "You know there's a backup? Her name is Barbara Morgan, and nobody will ever remember her."

"They will if they send her up on the next one."

"They won't. Once is enough. Like that nun who sang, Dominique." She killed herself last March, and it was barely in the newspaper except for one paragraph. Sister Smile. She lived with a woman after she stopped being a nun, but nobody was paying attention anymore."

She kept chattering, but then I heard someone moving in the bedroom and knew she was talking to cover up that Marvin was still here, that he hadn't gone home. "I'm going for a ride," I said, turning to glare at her.

She fumbled in her purse, her robe flapping open so I could see her sheer nightgown. "Treat yourself to McDonald's," she said, giving me a five-dollar bill."

"It's 10:30. I'm not hungry."

"You will be in an hour or so." I folded the bill and stuffed it in my pocket. "He'll be gone when you get back," she said. "I promise."

When I got my bike out of the garage we shared with the owner, I saw that Marvin had parked behind the house. I thought about dragging the key to my father's house along one panel to scratch it, but I rode straight to my father's with the key in my pocket. If he was gone, I was going into the house and into the bedroom, and so what if he came home then because I was frozen, even with a sweat shirt under my thin jacket, and I could tell him that getting warm was why I'd let myself in.

I saw his car in the driveway as I rode past and dropped the bike behind the forsythia. Right about now, I thought, my mother would be naked and counting on me to spend her money at McDonald's. I told myself she'd have the front door locked, something leaning against it so I'd make a racket if I came back early.

Sharon's curtains were as tightly closed as my father's. I knew she was at church and wouldn't be back until after twelve. She wasn't allowed to miss.

I walked half way up my father's driveway before I stepped onto the lawn in front of his bedroom window. I was shivering so much I wanted to wrap my arms around myself, but I put my hands on my hips as if I was about to speak.

I wondered if my father was looking from one of the other windows, but then I figured why would he be? I hadn't made any noise. He was more likely to step outside because he was leaving in his car.

I thought about shouting my father's name, calling out Frank like a friend stopped by, but I couldn't think of one reason somebody would show up and do that. I didn't know what to do except pick up a stone and imagine throwing it through his bedroom window.

If he looked out through the broken glass, I would ask him if he ever thought of my mother as he watched his videos, visualizing her body. I knew he'd probably just stare at me, not saying anything, but it didn't matter because I already knew the answer to that question. It was just that there seemed to be some small comfort in asking it.

Flying to Alaska

Roy Berndt struggles for a few seconds, hitching his wheelchair over the short step into my kitchen, and then he hand-drives it close to where I'm sitting. "Charley got me, that's for sure," he says. "He done me in." I ask Roy if he'd like a beer and he grins, but when he sees Molson on the label of the one I'm holding, he says, "Nothing foreign is all."

I glance at the label as if it's begun to glow. "Canada's not foreign."

"Don't tell me what I know," Roy says, and then he smiles again and rolls backward a few feet.

"It's ok," I say. "There's local."

I come back with a Yuengling, and he gives me a thumbs-up. "Thank you kindly."

I expect him to bring up the virtues of the brewery in Pottsville, a half hour away, but he wants to talk about the trees coming down the length of Galaxy Street. Do us all good, the politicians say, nothing huge and heavy, for starters, toppling into our bedrooms on a stormy night, but there's not much to see of the benefits they're claiming. The block of doubles we live on looks like two sets of row houses without the old maples and oaks. "Like a slum starting while we're sitting here," Roy observes, and I have to agree.

"Foreigners coming next," he adds, finally working that theme back into our talk. "You'll see. Take the trees down, you're inviting aliens."

"I'll be making room for a half double of them," I say, "if I quit my job and can't find another."

Roy drops his eyes to my breasts as if he's sizing up why I might quit being a waitress, what other kind of work I might get. I wait for him to start with "A girl like you . . ." but he lights a cigarette and takes a long, slow drag. "I know how you feel," he says, "the boss is always right."

"It's my own hassle to deal with," I say, but Roy's suddenly sitting up like a man who wants me to notice the body he has left--the size of his shoulders and arms, the swell of his chest. He looks like he's been weight training from the waist up every day for twenty years; he looks like somebody who thinks of nothing but making up for his lost legs, somebody who might come into my house and put his hands on me like a boss, looking in my eyes to see if what comes next is his choice or mine.

"I'm off," Roy says, handing me the already empty Yuengling. "You don't have to wait up for me." He blows me a kiss before he wheels himself down the driveway and into the street. It's five blocks to the American Legion where Roy goes every Wednesday night, and the sidewalk along both sides of Galaxy has heaved up over the years from all those trees. I imagine him returning in the dark, drunk where late traffic might run up on him despite the reflectors on the front and back of his chair.

WHEN ROY'S TWIN DAUGHTERS COME OUT on the porch ten minutes later, they're holding sparklers and matches. I put my empty Molson and the Yuengling in the sink and step back outside with a fresh Gold. Cheryl, Roy's girlfriend, is in the yard watching the girls squealing over their first sparks. "They can't wait for tomorrow," Cheryl says, and she brings her own drink across the driveway. "If they clean up, Roy won't know a thing. He's a stickler for the Fourth of July being the Fourth of July."

"I know how that is," I say. "My father wouldn't let me and my brothers touch a present until the sun came up on Christmas morning." I sit and stretch out, put my feet up on the porch wall. "Tan's coming along," Cheryl says, surprising me in the twilight.

"Good weather on my days off these last two weeks," I say.

"You ought to watch yourself laying out like you do and living alone here," Cheryl says. "There's plenty of eyes."

"Most everybody's at work," I say, though it's only been June and three days I've lived here, and I don't know anybody but Cheryl and Roy right next door, not counting the old woman who lives in the other half of my double.

"Roy's got eyes. It's only up to his knees that's gone."

"I can see that," I say, but I look at Cheryl's stomach and smile when she pats it. "Five months and starting to get in the way," she says. "Roy keeps saying 'boy' like saying makes it happen. He's all about fortune telling and such; he's got more spells and charms than a witch doctor, but nothing brings your legs back except strapping onto the stumps and standing."

Cheryl swallows her drink so fast I think she's got straight ginger ale. She smiles then and says, "Some day, before you know it, you'll feel yourself swelling up like this and forming dreams. Women have always felt like this when they're with child. It's science that kills dreams."

She looks at me so hard, I say, "I've never hear anyone use that expression."

"It's right there in the Bible. Mary and all the rest of them are with child. That's the way to say it, for sure. Even if your man is an asshole, that feeling is all yours. It has such a privacy that can't be changed."

The twins, I think, are writing their names with the sparklers. Dawn and Coral flash and go out--by next summer they'll be lounging on the porch steps looking for boys.

"Vietnam did awful things," I say.

Cheryl looks in her glass like she's trying to conjure it full again. "To some, maybe, but Roy lost his legs in a car crash," she says. "He's been telling that Vietnam story so long he thinks nobody remembers the truth."

"Wasn't he in the war?"

"Oh, sure he was, but he came home on two legs. Had them for a week before he got drunk and drove them away."

She's maybe thirty, I think. "That's twenty years or more ago," I say. "That's like when I was born."

"It don't matter none he lived up to Wilkes-Barre then. Word trickles down when you're under the same roof," Cheryl says. "I don't have to see things for myself to know. He's had your whole life on them stumps. You ponder on that, and you'll know why it's right to keep such goings on to yourself. It's a comfort to him, and I'm not up to pressing. There's no good can come of what's true."

Who do you decide to tell? I want to ask, but the girls returning to their porch swivels her head. "Coral, Dawn," she yells then, "pick the damn things up or your daddy's going to be pissed." She shakes her ice cubes. "Excuse me," she says, "business."

"Sure."

"Hey," she says, "you around tomorrow night?"

"Like always."

"Roy's got something. You come over. You'll love it."

To tell the truth, I want to explain to Cheryl I wish Roy had lost his legs in Vietnam because I already know one guy who lost his in a car, and the procedure is starting to sound as familiar as repetitive stress--you type until you get carpal tunnel syndrome; you drive until you lose your legs.

I rode in a car with that boy the night before he crashed. It gets you to thinking, like those old Greeks and Romans were right about fate and the furies.

THE 4TH TURNS OUT HOT AND SUNNY, too, so I put on my two-piece to catch an hour of it. In twenty minutes, when it's time to turn, I roll over and see Roy looking at me from a downstairs window. He doesn't back off from the open space. "You'll burn," he says. "Your skin's too fair for tanning."

I raise my head to answer and say "It's ok," lowering myself at once because I know he's staring at my breasts.

"You need to come over for some beers and burgers to keep yourself from cancer," he says, and I hear his wheelchair bump the wall, know, without glancing up again, that he's leaning forward through the space where anybody else would have a screen.

I lie still. For fifteen minutes, because I don't hear anything else but the gnats by my ears and traffic, I don't learn anything about Roy's eyes, but when I pick myself up, satisfied with my courage for staying outside, he's still in the window, and neither of us says anything while I stand up, knowing exactly where all of my tan lines are forming.

When I move toward the house, he shouts, "That's better. You ready for that beer now?"

I take my time showering and changing. I wear something sleeveless so Roy can't think I'm covering myself like a nun, and when I make my way across the alley, Cheryl is setting up the grill and there are six bottles lined up on the porch wall.

"Roy says you got boss problems," Cheryl says as soon as we all settle with our beers. "Is that what I think it is?"

"I tell myself it's not me," I say. "He comes on to all the waitresses; he looks at all of us."

"But you can't abide that," Cheryl says.

"I might," I say. "That's what I'm going to find out if I stay there."

Cheryl smiles like somebody caught anticipating what she is going to hear. She flicks her hair from her eyes to give her face time to change. "You shouldn't think that way," she says.

"I have to," I say.

"Well then, you shouldn't have to."

"No, I shouldn't," I say, but Cheryl's smile doesn't come back.

Roy lights a cigarette, and because he puts it down to reach for his beer, I notice he has an ashtray built into the arm rest of his wheelchair. He sees me looking and laughs, slipping into the wheeze of the heavy smoker. "Goddamn," he says, "and I used to be able to run like the wind."

"You don't need running for a reason to cut back," Cheryl says.

"Really," Roy says, "like the goddamned wind. Listen, do you know who won the Olympics in 1968, for women, the 100 meters?"

"No idea. That was before I was born."

"Wyomia Tyus," Roy says. "That was the year I graduated high school. And her time was 11.0."

Roy lifts his cigarette again. "Those coals are looking good, baby," he says. "You know what my time was in high school? 10.9, that's what it was. I would have won the Olympics for women."

Cheryl shrugs. "That's great, Roy," she says, but she's already moving up the ramp to the front door.

"You know who won in 1972?" Roy says. I shake my head. "Renate Stecher, that's who. Some German, some Commie, and her time wasn't even as good, so I would have won again except I wasn't on my feet by then."

Inside the house, Cheryl turns up the country radio station. A woman I don't recognize is singing about seeing her man with another woman during her lunch hour. She's deciding to break the news to him after work when Cheryl backs through the door with a plate of raw burgers and three more beers. The twins are right behind her, each of them with a soda.

We all drink fast for a few seconds, and then Cheryl slides the burgers off to the side of the fire like somebody trying to smoke ground meat. "The slower the song, the faster you drink," Roy says. "That's what bartenders will tell you."

"And the sadder the song, the more you drink," Cheryl adds, settling back down.

"But look here," Roy says, corralling the twins. "Ain't they something? And I got more where these came from." He holds on to the shoulders of the two girls. "Up to Alaska, another girl by an Eskimo."

"Roy sowed his oats," Cheryl says.

"I still see her when I want. She's not as get-gone as the mother of my sweethearts here."

Coral and Dawn act like they're deaf or like they've heard this story before; Roy looks like there's a camera pointed his way. "Don't start, Roy," Cheryl says. "She'll think you're the loony man."

"Out-of-the-body travel," Roy says. "I fly there--that Eskimo woman taught me good. It's better than walking."

I think, finishing my second beer, that the twins look like the daughters of nobody in particular, as if any woman within wheelchair range could have left them behind. "You got yourself your new legs," Cheryl says. "You can start walking again any time you want."

"The army can have my old ones. They're bought and paid for my own damn way, but they can stick them on somebody shows up empty-pants from the Gulf," Roy says. "Let that poor fuck learn the joy of walking like a retard. These pissant wars—they make people think shit's easy and nobody needs a damn thing coming home."

I nod to keep things going toward clarity, but Cheryl sits up and says, "Roy's never taken to his old legs, but he's done some good in designing the new ones. That's why he's getting back on his feet."

I try to imagine Roy as engineer, how he might have pressed his drawings and specs into the hands of a technician. Roy looks away from us for a few seconds, and then he says, "You don't have knees, you start understanding them good. It's not nothing you wouldn't learn if you were doing without."

"He'll show you, if he gets a mind to," Cheryl says. "They're a wonder."

"Girls," Roy says to the twins, "you get us three more of these good deeds and find something to do until the burgers are up."

Coral and Dawn fly inside and back out with the beer and a new batch of sparklers. "In the daytime?" Cheryl says, but Roy waves them off.

"They'll get something special in a couple of hours," he says.

Cheryl puts her beer down like I do this time, and Roy stubs out his cigarette before he lights another. "Burgers," he says, and finally Cheryl shoves them over so they sit above the coals. "You know what Cheryl's going to cook up for us in November?"

"No idea," I repeat, thinking four months is a long time to look forward to a meal.

"She's going to eat her placenta. She says it's full of vitamins and such because it keeps the baby healthy for all those months. She has a book that tells all about it." He laughs like it's hilarious, but it sounds like the way that boy who lost his legs laughed when the police pulled us over the night before his crash, short and breathy like someone trying to warm his hands.

"A placenta is sacred food," Cheryl says, "if you let the meat tell you how to prepare it for the fire."

I listen to the hamburger to hear its wishes, but not a word is getting through. Nothing about the browning meat seems the least bit sacred. "Placenta is a rare privilege for most of us," Cheryl says then, as if she's quoting again, and I can see why Roy is nervous.

"You can eat it raw or fried or in a stew," Cheryl says. "Even vegetarians can eat it because nothing has to be killed."

"Raw, for Christ's sake," Roy says, "you could give yourself AIDS if you eat the wrong fresh mother."

"It's not that unusual," I say. "They were going to do a skit about placenta eating on *Saturday Night Live* once."

"You're putting me on," Roy says. Sitting down like he is, and so close to the grill, there's a chance the flames flaring up from the spattering grease might catch his face.

"No. It got censored. It never got on the air. There was a product they were advertising called Placenta Helper. Dan Ackroyd or somebody was going to say, "Lets you stretch your placenta into a tasty casserole.""

Roy laughs until he wheezes. "That's funny as hell," he finally manages. Why'd they censor it?"

"The same reason they didn't do one on Amputation Barbeque," Cheryl says.

Roy laughs and coughs again, reaching for his beer. "You ought to be writing these down," he says, his voice thin.

"They hired a diviner out to Penn's Springs," Cheryl says. "They're paying him good money to find water."

"With a stick?" I say.

"Hazel," Roy says. "It can't just be a stick."

"See?" Cheryl says. "Roy believes in his magic, but he says he'll shoot me if I put that placenta anywhere near his mouth."

"It's woman's magic," Roy says. "It'll make a man weak. You got to know the sense of what you're believing."

Cheryl snorts. She goes back to her beer finally, and then she turns the burgers.

Roy put his cigarette and beer down at the same time. "All those years stumbling on those cheap legs. I felt like a man on life support or some such shit as that."

"Technology," I say. "We get hooked up to machines instead of priests."

Roy skids forward in his chair until it looks as if he intends to eat right off the grill. "Exactly," he says. "And if them things don't work like they oughta, we give up hope."

"This is old, baby," Cheryl says. "We're past this."

"You and the rest of everybody still got all their parts," Roy says, sounding like that lost-leg boy I knew when I said goodbye to him in his hospital room, but Cheryl's already busy with the burgers, slapping them onto a plate and calling in the twins.

"AIN'T THESE MOSQUITOES SOMETHING?" Roy says an hour later, Cheryl off to buy more beer, and I follow him inside. "So what's to do now?" he says, and I wait for him to work up his own answer.

"Look here," he finally says, wheeling himself over to the couch and waving me forward to see what's lying there. The legs look like they've been polished, and each of them has a painting detailed on the calf. Snakes and ivy and roses spiral down from knee to ankle, but Roy wants me to examine the inside of the knee. "There's things in the knee you don't know you have. It's a miracle is what it is; I put these on and I can run to Alaska. I want you be here when I strap on them legs."

I want to ask why he didn't strap them on the second he brought them home, but I remember to ask, "I thought you had to do therapy and all that before you could wear artificial legs."

"I walked on plastic before," Roy says at once. "I can remember."

How long ago was that? is the next question I want to ask, but I offer, "Great, so when's the big day?"

"You'll see," Roy says. "When I just walk over to your house and surprise you."

"There you go."

"When I put them on, I'll be standing tall. I won't take no shit from nobody. I'll be geared up and ready for battle."

I lift one of the legs, astonished by how light it is. "You could fly if all your parts were this light," I say.

"Exactly," Roy says, but he takes back the leg and lays it parallel to the other one. "Sometimes," he says, "I'd like to think of a way to hurt people that wouldn't stick."

While I puzzle over that, I look at the leg again, follow the snakes and flowers as if they led to where Roy had just gone. "Like war games?" I try.

Roy blinks. "One on one," he says. "Real pain before they get better. Killing them before they get up again."

He stops, but I don't say anything. "You thinking I'm an asshole," he says then.

"No," I say. "No, I don't," knowing I mean it.

"Well, I am," he says, "thank you anyway. Look at my legs, and here I am with a gun in every room, every one of them loaded." He leans so far forward in his chair I think he is going to tumble to the floor or grope me for balance. "It's a terrible thing to know who you are," he says. "You can't unstick that. For sure, you can't."

I decide, when he catches himself, that the only person Roy will ever shoot is himself. And then I think of other things besides guns he could use to kill me until I got up again, and I feel myself going wet under my arms and along my hairline.

WHEN CHERYL COMES BACK WITH THE TWINS and two six packs, she glances from Roy to those legs and back again. "You got that Eskimo look on your face, Roy. You going, Roy? You flying to Alaska?"

"You oughtna be saying some such as that," he says. "You might be breaking a spell."

Cheryl sits down on the couch beside the legs, sliding into one corner to give them room. "These are my special present to Roy," she says. "He stopped wearing those old legs right after I moved in last year, so after I got pregnant, I just had to make sure he was going to be up and around when the baby came."

Roy pushes back a bit in his chair, and when I turn he's staring out the window as if something important is outside. "Did Roy go on to you about him doing drawings and such about how to make the knee joint better? He was so excited he gave a copy to the place that makes these things." She pauses, but neither Roy nor I say anything. "Well," she goes on, "Roy's gone and done his with-the-new-leg time at the hospital. It's putting them on here inside the house these past weeks has him stymied."

I hear Roy's chair begin to move, and I take one side step as if I expect him to be aiming at me from behind. "Look here," he says, already half way to the kitchen, and Cheryl pushes herself up, the legs jostling against each other as she leaves them behind. We all follow him, but when he opens the package he pulls from the refrigerator, the twins say, "Gross" and run outside.

"Beef liver is all," Roy says. "Cheryl gets this stuff discount from the Bi-Lo where she works."

The meat glistens on the butcher paper. Roy spreads the liver out and rubs his hands across it. "Look here," he says. "Look at these veins. You see that pattern? It means you can't be sure what's coming."

I think I can see exactly that in the particle board the paper is lying on. It looks like the television when the cable goes out, when I don't know if it's weather, mechanical failure, or atomic war that's shut it off.

"Look here, though," Roy says. "See how it peaks there in that lobe, like a house roof? And over here, too. That's good; that's real good."

"Good how?" I try, because Cheryl appears to be transfixed.

"It says 'keep on with things.'"

I feel like I'm in church. I hold my bottle with both hands like a hymnal, and everything on the label repeats Roy's conclusion. "I tell the future by examining animal organs," he says. "Vein markings. Ridges. Fat. Shapes and colors."

"So, what are we doing, Roy?" Cheryl asks. "Are we going to eat this?"

Roy pokes at the meat, his head bowed as if he expects a preview of the rest of the evening. "I'll tell you what," he says, lifting his head, "I'll eat that placenta of yours if you let me read it first."

"Are you serious?"

I watch Roy to see, but he pushes on. "Armies moved because of what animal livers said," he says. "Generals waited for a reading."

"OK, Roy," Cheryl says, and though it's hard to tell what she means by that, I see Roy softening as if he's giving in to something.

Cheryl smiles. "You don't believe in any of this, do you?" she says to me.

"It's a challenge," I say.

"Don't be making him small," Cheryl says, her smile flattening.

"Ok."

It makes me small, too."

And though I nod then, I think it is a foolish thing to believe, attaching yourself to someone in a way that burdens you. Which is when Coral and Dawn walk in with a bag they each have hold of. "It's dark," they say together. "For real."

"Pinwheels," Roy says, looking through the window as if the twilight has taken him by surprise. "Wait'll you see this," he says. "I told the girls as soon as it starts getting dark."

He leaves the liver on the table, and we go back outside like it makes sense to forget the mosquitoes we couldn't stand twenty minutes ago. Dawn and Coral split up and go to work on opposite sides of the street, each of them tying a firecracker to one of the stumps the town has left behind. In a few seconds, Dawn and Coral move almost simultaneously away from us, setting up firecrackers on the next pair of stumps. "The girls know how to wire them down," Roy says. "They get a kick out of it."

"It's like they're in the army," I say, and Roy shoots me a look that makes me take a swallow of the warm beer I've been nursing since Cheryl left.

Roy waits until Dawn and Coral finish another pair. "They got girls what do things now," he finally says. "Surely they do, the army, goddamn it."

"Sorry," I say.

"For what?" he says. "I just thought you were reading my mind there when I was thinking of taking a gun to things before they got too big to kill." He looks at the girls, who are at the far end of the block fixing the last two stumps. "You think that's crazy talk?" he says.

"It could be. It depends."

"Goddamn right it depends. Goddamn right about that."

The girls run our way. "When Daddy?" Coral says. "When do we set off the street?"

Cheryl steps outside, and I'm happy to see she's carrying only one full beer. She's put on a fresh blouse and combed her hair so it falls neatly to the side when she lays the bottle against Roy's palm. Roy smiles. "Crazy talk is all," he says. "It comes from sitting too long." He turns to the twins. "As soon as I get my lips around this here bottle," he says. "And then it's bombs away."

Roy takes such a long pull, his bottle goes more empty than the ones Cheryl and I have been nursing. "Ready?" Cheryl says.

"Go," Roy says, and the girls run to our right, setting matches, I can tell, to fuses that reach the ground. "I got it all timed," Roy says, "each fuse is shorter than the last, and the last ones give the girls time to get back to the porch," but just after Dawn and Coral light the last fuses, the firecrackers farthest to our right snap and crackle and burst into spirals.

"Goddamn," Roy says. "Goddamn it all," and then, right as the girls finish sprinting back to us the rest of the fireworks go off almost simultaneously.

"Shit, yes," Roy hollers, "We got pinwheels," and Cheryl and the twins and I whoop as well, the neighbors coming out in small bunches to watch sixteen pinwheels, eight on each side of the street, spinning white on the stumps like crazed luminaria, fizzing and spitting sparks, the five of us yelling as if our voices could make them last, keeping them going like they were run by batteries. Just after the last one goes out, we can hear applause from all the porches.

"That was something," Cheryl says.

"Pinwheels." Roy says. "They're the shit."

"If he had both legs he'd be king pisser," Cheryl says, but I can tell she doesn't expect anything from me now, so I can keep my thinking to myself. "You cook me up that liver," Roy says "It's full of strength. I've decided I'm wearing those legs tonight."

"All right, Roy," Cheryl says. "Ok, baby." She pushes him inside, but when I follow behind the girls, it comes to me that he might be less than something with both legs. The same way I'd be worse for having more than the plain face and large breasts I take to work every day.

In the kitchen Cheryl puts her hands on Roy's shoulders and rubs them. "You won't have to swallow me raw, baby," she says.

None of us say anything. In all that quiet, the liver looks so small, suddenly, I imagine it couldn't support a cow, and as soon as I think that, it turns horrible, and I wish I'd never tried to humor Roy, that I had the courage to name the things I know are stupid and dangerous to believe in.

Roy reaches up finally and puts his hands on hers. She leans down and whispers something into his ear and he laughs.

"Another beer while I'm waiting," he says.

"Sure, baby." Cheryl puts her tongue in his ear, but he doesn't seem to notice.

"Onions," he says, poking at the liver, hefting it in his hands.

Cheryl is groping under his shirt. "Tobasco," he says, holding the liver up so close to his face I think he's going to sink his teeth into it.

And then Cheryl laughs once, her face still beside his, before she slaps a pan on the stove and drops the liver with a soft thwap and I stand, back toward the door, and let myself out so quietly I might never have been there at all.

There are limits, and we are something regardless. And what we aren't keeps us from leaving ourselves, which is what I want to tell Roy, though I don't, of course, even when, from the dark of my living room, I see him trying out his new legs a half hour later. He lurches and holds on to Cheryl. I hear him cursing, the window still open so I think of the insects entering that kitchen, coming to the light. "Ok, baby," I hear Cheryl say. "Ok." And then I have to imagine what else she might be saying because a car pulls up across the street, double parking, its radio turned up so loud the rest of the night's sounds are smothered by it. Roy passes back and forth where I can see him through the kitchen window, expecting him, each time he turns my way, to believe he's crossed a border, that he's walked far enough to enter my house and learn which parts of my body have the power of spells, or if, I think then, any of them are potent at all.

Human Subject

WAYNE SCHUCK HAS BEEN A HUMAN SUBJECT BEFORE. He's managed a week of low-salt followed by a week of high-salt while women in lab coats took blood samples. He's taken pills both easy and hard to swallow and let himself be watched and measured. He's been happy and angry, but mostly fogged up or what he thinks is unchanged. Just once, he's felt his heart race in a way that made him get up and walk for an hour because he was sure he would die if he stopped moving. No one ever tells him what they've learned from observing him. He gets his check and signs out as someone witnesses his signature and enters the date and time. If any of the stuff he's taken has given him permanent damage, he can't tell. If any of it will cause him a problem years from now, he isn't thinking that far ahead.

This time the trial is housed at an out-of-business motel Wayne has passed a hundred times. He almost misses the turn because he's so used to the lot being empty that he doesn't recognize it nearly full of cars. Shivering, he checks his watch and sees he is getting in just under deadline. June 3rd, he thinks, walking across the lot, and so chilly I can see my breath.

Although it is 8:58, there are seven guys in each registration line. All men this time, Wayne decides. Some sort of Viagra, maybe. Something where you have to worry about keeping a hard-on for half a day when something goes wrong. The man who moves up across from Wayne wears a t-shirt that says *Life sucks and so should you.* The guy in front of him has one of those Christian fish symbols on the back of his shirt. Wayne wants to tell both of them that he's never even owned a bumper sticker, let alone a shirt that talks, but he doesn't want glares from both heaven and hell.

Wayne recognizes all of the forms—liability release, informed consent, privacy statement, and payment method. "You're employed full time?" a young woman says, sounding as if he she thinks he's lied.

"Yes."

She opens her hands in front of her like an apology. "I'm sorry if I implied anything," she says. "It's just that nearly all of our subjects are unemployed or students."

"And I don't look like a student?"

The young woman looks like she's in college, maybe getting credit for doing this work. "You'll be isolated," she says. "You'll have no interaction with anyone except staff members for twelve days." Wayne nods and signs on four lines. He is a "healthy volunteer" for this one. Two weeks on the science clock instead of taking the vacation the grocery gives him. A double-blind comparison. He might receive the placebo, a thought that relaxes him until he sees his room doesn't have a television.

"Don't you worry about that," the young man who's escorted him says. "We'll keep you busy." Wayne feels him watching as he examines Room 208. The bed is bare, the mattress yellowed as if slept on by years of sweating bodies. A set of white sheets and a pillowcase sit on the gray, damp-looking pillow. Wayne hangs up three shirts in the small closet. The dresser drawers are empty except for a faded, bald tennis ball that looks chewed. A dog's toy, Wayne thinks. He doesn't touch it, nor does he put any of his jeans, t-shirts, underwear, and socks in that drawer.

The young man leads Wayne to a room to be interviewed and tested by the first person Wayne's seen who looks old enough to be any kind of doctor. He rearranges shapes to make circles and squares and rectangles. He selects one of five answers about choices he'd make under a variety of stresses. He recognizes a reflex test he's taken twice before. After he's finished, he's handed two yellow oblong pills. "Your room has been examined while you've been here," the test-giver says. "I want you to understand that. We have to be certain you won't ingest anything that will interfere with the test."

"It was on the form," Wayne says. "I know about all this."

"A veteran," the man says. "So you know your person will be searched as well."

"Someone will always be in the hall on your floor if you feel anxious," another young woman says. "Help yourself to some magazines or puzzle books. There is an exercise room that still has the old equipment in it. Someone will be in there to keep you from talking to other subjects, but you're welcome to take advantage. Exercise doesn't affect our study. The pool, however, is empty." For a moment, Wayne believes she is going to escort him and do the body search, but that thought disappears as soon as the young man steps into the doorway and gestures him back to 208.

"I must ask you to fully disrobe," he says. Wayne faces away from him as he undresses. He is so cold he feels his genitals shrivel to humiliation size.

Alone again, Wayne dresses and wraps himself in the one flimsy blanket lying at the foot of the bed. Though 208 has a balcony, the sliding glass door that leads to it is locked from outside. In the tiny bathroom, one towel and a washcloth are folded beside the sink. A tan stain spreads in a fading spiral from the drain. There is a similar stain in the bathtub. The faucet, when he turns it on, coughs out brown water for a few seconds, and then it clears. His dinner is delivered to his door, which isn't locked, but just like the girl has promised, there is someone with a bouncer's build in the hall. He lies on the bed and looks at the ceiling for two hours until the same burly man knocks and leads him back to the test room. "It's like being on jury duty," the attendant says. "We don't want you tainting yourselves by mingling and revealing how you feel." This time Wayne grabs a Sudoku puzzle book, 100 of them graded from beginner to expert. "Hours and hours of fun," the cover says. Wayne notices that all the easy ones, numbers 1-25, are filled in. The rest are untouched except #100. *Ultra Hard*, it says at the top of the page. Six numbers are filled in. A half dozen more squares show erasures that have worked holes through the paper.

It looks to Wayne as if he will have plenty of time to think. That's what his mother would say to justify sitting around doing nothing for hours while yellow pills do their work. "Use your time to your advantage if you're going to be a guinea pig," she said when he told her last week what he was doing for his vacation. "You can work things out with yourself while you're doing someone else's job."

"I can't stand anything I hear myself thinking."

"You sound like your father when you talk like that."

"Dad always sounded neutral."

"That's exactly what I mean. He's a hundred miles away, but I can hear him right this minute in my ear."

HE'D BEEN CUTTING HER GRASS AND TRIMMING her shrubbery. After his father left, she'd refused to move away from a house and yard too big to manage. "You can still help," she'd said when Wayne had finally moved out, too. "You're not going a hundred miles like your father." For eight years now, he'd done the lawn and landscaping. "Your father," she said every summer, "if he ever drives by, will see it's perfect."

That afternoon, after he turned down her iced tea offer, she'd poured him a glass anyway. When he pushed it into the middle of the patio table, she'd said, "You're so angry. Until those girls, you never used to be so angry." She meant him to consider his recently broken engagement. His third one. "All within two years," she said. "How is that possible?"

"I wanted the hat trick," he said, and his mother clicked her tongue.

"Honest to Pete. You're smarter than that, Wayne. There's your father again saying, 'We all have to take our medicine' like he was wrapped up in those chains the way that ghost in the old Christmas story was. I can hear him clanking when you talk like that."

"Not so smart that I'm working check-out at the grocery."

She picked up the glass of tea and sipped. When he frowned, she said, "There's no sense in you smothering yourself with that sort of thinking."

"I have to go," he said. "The yard will dazzle Dad if he picks today to make the two-hour drive."

His mother stood between Wayne and his car. "When I go through your line at the store, you know every vegetable and piece of fruit they sell there, even the okra and the fresh spices and all those things that look like roots. None of the other checkers know. 'What's that?' they ask me, as if lettuce only comes in the shape of a ball, and I always want to tell them it's something really cheap, some kind of cabbage, but I just can't even though they deserve it."

"Once we're on the job six months, we all get paid the same, Mom. I got the two weeks vacation because I've finished two years now."

"People will notice. You'll see."

"They already did, Mom. After a month, they started calling me Mr. Produce."

"You're only thirty-two. That's not old, not these days. Forty's the new thirty. You have eight more years to be young unless all those things you let people feed you are doing something to ruin you right this minute."

"I don't always take the real stuff, Mom," but it didn't stop her from rattling on while they stood in her driveway for another ten minutes.

His mother always forgot about the tests without drugs like the week he spent being examined for "Shift Work Disorder" back when he was working in the grocery warehouse, alternating day and night shift. He was unhappy every day, but he'd never thought he had a disorder. Extra money, though, was extra money, and all he had to do was tell the truth. Out front in the grocery, he was still on shifts, but the difference between 8-4:30 and 12:30 to 9 was the problem of getting his feet on the floor at 7 a.m. every other week.

This morning, just after eight o'clock, while he was longing for the coffee he'd had the night before, his last cup for nearly two weeks, his mother had called. "This might be the last time you're normal," she said.

"I've never had any of those things they say really fast in the TV ads, Mom."

"Numbness in the limbs," she said. "Muscular weakness, swelling of the lips and tongue. See your doctor immediately."

"No four-hour erection?"

She made her clicking sound before she said, "Everybody knows that's impossible, so when it never happens those drug companies can pat themselves on the back like they're selling miracles."

"Somebody had one, Mom. Trust me."

His mother sighed as if he'd brought home a rumor about his second-grade teacher. "That's what they said about Jesus on Easter."

"You'll make me late," Wayne said. He stared at the clock, choosing a time three minutes away when he would say "I have to go" and hang up.

"It's not too late to remind you it's a good thing you were born in 1981 and not 1961," she said. "I'm talking about Thalidomide. Those women who took it, they had babies with flippers for arms and legs; they had kids who had hands coming out of their shoulders. Don't you ever worry that your babies one day will have burdens to bear?"

"It doesn't look like that's ever going to be a concern."

"Don't do that hangdog act. It's not attractive in a man. You ever talk to your father on the phone? You'd think you'd just seen your first-born son with toes sticking out of his ankles. What were they thinking, those women who trusted people who wanted to sell them something to make their lives easier?"

"Back then," Wayne said, "the people who volunteered for the tests just showed up and took things. They didn't have a piece of paper to remind them that something could go wrong."

"Just because people are willing doesn't make it right. These rules they have to follow now should have been written down a hundred years ago when pills first got made. Or maybe two hundred or whenever it was pills and medicine started. Whenever anybody who invented something wanted the world to use it."

"I have to go, Mom."

"Sure you do," she said and hung up before Wayne had a chance to push *End Call*.

Now Wayne rubs his hands together and hugs himself, shivering. He looks to where someone renting this room would expect to see a coffee maker, but the counter is bare. He bets himself that counter was bare at least a year before the motel had closed. A moment later, he bets himself they haven't counted on a day this cold in June, what with the heat long since turned off.

HIS FIRST JOB WAS WHEN HIS FATHER, a janitor for the school district, got him hired for the summer. "Remember who you want people to think you are," his father said as they walked into the school Wayne had attended until the week before, and then, at 7:15, Wayne held a putty knife and lay down to scrape the underside of the high school gym's bleachers. "This will take you a while," the foreman said, and left.

Wayne had sat on those bleachers a hundred times. He'd stuck his share of boogers under his seat during ninth grade, giving it up when the longing for girls drove him to manners. In three months, Wayne had told the foreman, he was beginning college. "Well, until then," the foreman had said, and Wayne understood this scraping was the kind of job summer help got stuck with—unskilled and awful—what the full-time janitors would never do as long as there was a budget for hiring on summer help. He thought of urinals and toilets, what might be caked under the rims of each and how he would be instructed to clean them.

Summer, his father had told him, was when schools recovered from injuries, but all morning the job carved its initials in the air, spray-painted the *eat-me* and *fuck-you* of contempt. In the supply closet, Wayne found the extra-duty cleaner and a couple of rags because tiny obscenities were inked in the spaces between the wood slats--three ways to enter Courtney, a name Wayne couldn't match to a face; five ways to kill Mr. Wallace, an English teacher he'd had as a sophomore; and in a font that resembled Italics, what someone wanted to do again and again to Miss Kane, who'd been hired, apparently, after being a student teacher during Wayne's last semester.

Wayne was making "Robbie Kirkland is a faggot" smear and disappear when he heard the foreman shout, "Schuck!" He was on his feet before he understood it was his father the foreman was talking to. "Get the fucking lead out," the foreman said, sounding as if he was in the adjacent lobby, but Wayne couldn't hear his father's response. "What am I looking at here?" the foreman started up again. "Tell me so I can treasure it."

Nothing else. The foreman's voice shut off like a radio.

At lunch, an hour later, his father looked the same, eating his sandwich and his apple, going to the fountain once for a drink of water. "How's it going?" his father finally said.

"I can see why the teachers never wanted us to chew gum."

"That job is everybody's first day," his father said. "In a few days, you'll be on your feet like the rest of us."

All afternoon Wayne lay flat on his back, soundless, scraping gum and snot, erasing a year's worth of insults and wishful thinking. Ten minutes before it was time to punch out, the foreman showed up to inspect Wayne's work with a mirror on a stick, grading like a dentist. As if he'd scouted, the foreman went right to where a cluster of obscenities had been printed. "See you tomorrow, kid," the foreman said, tapping the mirror against Wayne's chest before he said, "Go and clock out. There sure as fuck's no overtime on this job."

Wayne and his father punched out with the rest of the crew, the foreman following them through the lobby toward the main door. "Wait for me by the car," his father said, but Wayne opted, after a minute in the full sun of June, for the shade of the front door's overhang. Inside, he could see his father kneeling to take scuff marks from the lobby wall. Before he could be seen, Wayne walked back to the car and stood in the sun.

He waited for eight minutes, his back turned to the sun that shone over the roof of the high school from a cloudless sky. "That wasn't so bad, was it?" his father called from what sounded like fifty feet away.

"What wasn't?" Wayne said at once, but when he turned, squinting into the sun, his father's expression was fixed as if he hadn't heard.

"Ok?" his father said, closing up the distance. "You ok?" and Wayne laid his bare arms across the car roof and gave his father a thumbs-up sign with both hands, holding it as long as he could against the heat.

The last girl he'd lived with, his third fiancée, had left to go back to a community college where her parents lived sixty miles away. She was going to be a nurse. "I can't do this anymore," she said, gesturing toward the aisles of the grocery.

Looking down the rows of canned goods with her, Wayne wanted to tell her there were worse jobs. He'd delivered pizzas. Clerked at a convenience store. And worst, he'd been a dishwasher in an *open 24 hours* diner, lasting one day listening to everybody in the back room speak Spanish.

He didn't go back to get his money for the eight hours. He kept hearing what always sounded like jabber, and knew that somewhere in those sounds would be phrases that laughed at him--"The silent gringo" or "the pale motherfucker with the soft hands"--some joke that he didn't want to have translated.

Wayne hadn't said anything as she nodded at a sign that read "salty snack foods" before she went on. "And I can't make a commute like that in order to stay here," all it took to let him know his place in her future. A ring, thank God, was still just a promise he'd made.

"They're starting one of those community colleges around here in a year or two," Wayne had said as if that was any kind of argument. It was like packing her suitcase for her.

IT IS NEARLY MIDNIGHT WHEN WAYNE PULLS the single hard backed chair up to the locked balcony door. He has a view of the parking lot and the Interstate. He is looking north, Wayne knows that much.

Wayne remembers that there is a Dutch Pantry less than a quarter mile to the west that he'd be able to see if he could get outside. He's eaten there once with his mother, and though the food was unremarkable, he'd loved playing a peg game that sat beside the salt and pepper shakers on the table. It was a version of solitaire, jumping one peg over another, removing each jumped peg until, if you did it exactly right, there would be just one peg left. Wayne ended up with three, then two, then four and three again just as their orders arrived. "Almost," his mother kept saying. He ate a hot turkey sandwich and French fries and watched his mother fuss with a ham slice, nicking off tiny edges of fat until she gave up and ordered a slice of shoo-fly pie, giving him a few minutes to play three more times, leaving two pegs twice. "You're getting so good at that," his mother said, half the pie still sitting on her plate.

Wayne replaced all of the pegs and pushed the board across the table. "Oh no," she said. "You're the expert."

"You never know."

His mother jumped the pegs without seeming to pay attention, but a few minutes later, she ended up with two pegs. "Beginner's luck," she said as the waitress approached.

"You'll get it down to one peg after a few tries," the waitress said. "You through with that pie?"

"Oh no," his mother said, covering it for a second with her hands. "Wrap it up for me."

"I'll finish it," Wayne said. He took the pie in one hand and the game in the other. The waitress shrugged and laid the check on the table. Three bites and the pie was gone. "I'll buy you one of these for Christmas," Wayne said, dropping a few dollars on the table beside the game board and getting up with the check in his hand.

He wishes he had that game right now. He'd have eleven days to figure out the pattern. If he won the very first day, he'd ask what was in the yellow pills.

He gets up and presses his face against the glass, trying to see the restaurant, but now that he thinks about it, that Dutch Pantry has shut down just like the motel he is in. He backs away from the door when he sees the two young women walking to a car parked in what he knows is the handicap zone just outside the front door. Despite the closed glass door, he can hear them laughing, and when the car starts, a song he doesn't recognize roars from the speakers, disappearing, a few seconds later, toward where that abandoned Dutch Pantry stands.

He lies on the bed and picks up the puzzle book, turning to #99, but that one is ruined from all the erasures on the other side of the page. He stares at #98, trying to figure it in his head because he doesn't have a pen or a pencil. His father left before anyone in the family ever heard of Sudoku. His mother thinks Sudoku is silly. And anyway, the answers are in the back of the book, so she wouldn't be impressed, especially with #100 not being finished.

What his mother thinks is important are all those release forms and privacy pledges, the things that made you consider what sorts of danger you might be in. Whether this was an adventure that anyone could do like skydiving, where all you need to do is fall.

"Pay no attention to anything you see or hear in this place," his father had said to Wayne that summer a month before he'd packed two suitcases and three liquor store boxes and left, but Wayne had kept looking and listening. He still felt his father's breath on the back of his neck while the store manager unlocked his register when his shift ended. Or in the way women watched the prices he rang up, their suspicion. Or worse, in the way they clutched their coupons, the ones they carried like medicine.

He is still awake at two a.m., but he convinces himself the insomnia is from first-night jitters. His ears are ringing. Not exactly ringing, more like a high-pitched buzz, as if he can hear an alarm that is sounding inside a locked building half a mile away. If he has this for more than a few weeks, it will be maddening. He will never be able to be alone in a quiet place.

Unusual thoughts. He remembers the phrase from the side-effect list in a commercial for a pain killer. *Confusion. Fear.* Wasn't everyone confused and afraid? Didn't they have unusual thoughts?

He stands and leans against the glass door, watching the thruway and remembering the boy in a nearby town who stepped into the path of a truck a few miles from this motel. Because he was bullied at school for being effeminate. Because everybody thought he was gay. Wayne tells himself *suicidal thoughts* is a side effect, but *suicide* is something different altogether.

The squeal in his ears stops. Wayne tears the answer pages out of the paperback and tosses them on the floor. He will borrow a pencil tomorrow. Nobody will worry that he might gouge his eyes out. And nobody will care whether he walks off with the book after he signs himself out. He pages back to the beginning and rips out the page that says *Answers to each puzzle begin on page 102.*

The Eternal Language of the Hands

Crossed Hands

When Uncle Teddy died just after vomiting blood in the upstairs toilet at my grandfather's house, my mother lectured me about the power of cancer, what smoking three packs of cigarettes a day will do to your throat and lungs. "He brought that filthy habit home from the war," she said, "and now look at him, barely thirty and gone." I was six, expected to be quiet and listen. I didn't say anything about how I was glad Uncle Teddy was dead, that his artificial voice box scared me more than the black leather belt he used, even after he'd gotten sick, on my cousin Tim, who was eight, for being "a Goddamned pest."

Uncle Teddy was laid out in a silk-lined casket in my grandfather's living room. Because of all the flowers and the chairs set up for Aunt Rhonda and Tim and his three sisters, there was space for only two or three people at a time to look at him. By the second day, everybody knew to move to the kitchen at 1:15 to eat lunch because not one person had come to the viewing at that time the day before. Nobody who was at work had a lunch hour then; nobody would stop that early on the way to the 3 to 11 shift at the mill four blocks away. Aunt Rhonda and all the rest settled themselves with ham sandwiches and potato salad. My mother, after fixing me a sandwich, told me not to spill my glass of milk. "Where do you think your Aunt Rhonda came by that bottle of beer?" she whispered to me as if I might know the answer. When she sat down beside my father, I laid my plate and cup on the counter and left the kitchen to go to the bathroom.

I had to pass through the room where Uncle Teddy was laid out.

He looked different with nobody else around, and that's when I leaned over the side of the casket and touched Uncle Teddy's hands that were folded just above where his dark suit coat was buttoned over his chest. They weren't any more scary than the hands of my sister's dolls, but my cousin Tim walked in while I was feeling Uncle Teddy's fingers and shouted, "You little turd," and I let go a stream of urine in my pants because I thought he'd tell Aunt Rhonda, and then everybody would hate me for being a Goddamned pest.

"Serves you right," he said, and I ran upstairs and locked myself in the bathroom. I took off my pants and briefs and hung them in the open window. When I sat on the closed toilet, it felt like Uncle Teddy's hands spread across my bare butt, and I remembered Tim pulling down his pants one afternoon to show me his welts from Uncle Teddy's belt. He told me to touch where the buckle had left a mark. "I bet you couldn't take it," he said. "You'd cover your ass with your hands and cry."

A half hour later, when my mother said, "Open up," my pants were still soaked. "What's wrong with you?" she said, and when I didn't answer, she told me to pull those pants on, piss or no piss, and she balled up the briefs in my hand, saying "Don't you dare drop them," and walked me to the three rooms we rented six blocks away. "Your best Sunday pants," she said when we reached our apartment. "The stink will never come out."

Right-Handed

The summer Tim's sister Kathy, who was a year younger than me, died from leukemia, I gripped her coffin right-handed and lifted, my other male cousins and I taking so little of the weight the funeral director and his brother lifted from either end to keep us from falling.

I was nine, the youngest. Tim was twelve by then; the oldest of those cousins was fifteen. I'd never heard the word pall-bearer before, but as soon as my mother had clipped on my tie and straightened the sport coat Tim had worn until six months before, I knew I was going to be closely watched.

I'd been smart enough to choose the side that let me use my right hand and arm. I knew enough about my body to understand my left hand would pull the weight of a six-year-old. We slid that coffin along a set of rails into a hearse, and then my cousins and I were directed by the funeral director's look to the leather couches of an enormous car. Inside the fingers of my right hand, a white groove darkened to red, then vanished, while silence shouldered among us until Kathy was absence.

The last time I'd seen Kathy she'd looked as pale as the angel my mother said she was becoming. "Heaven's waiting," she said after we'd seen her hold both of her hands against her head as if she was listening closely for the breath of God as he ran toward her. But the morning of the funeral, among my cousins in that limousine, I became a boy who believed we were all of us left out when it came to eternity.

The black-suited driver watched us in the mirror, and Tim kept his sunglasses on, ones that looked so much like the kind Ray Charles wore, the driver might have thought he was blind. I tried, each time his eyes flicked over and up, to stare what I'd learned about the impossibility of God into his memory. There was a war the United States hadn't won just ended in Korea. The Communists, according to my father, were sneaking closer while we slept. "People have their eyes closed shut," he said. "They think losing everything is inconceivable." I added it to my list of the in-words he used when he was angry: incomplete, incurable, inconsolable, incensed.

As if I'd stolen them from my mother's black handbag, I kept those words to myself, afraid to spend them.

The Platitudes of Handwork

During the year that followed, I began to learn that my father's advice to always "just put one foot in front of the other" wasn't original with him. He borrowed from the public domain of mottoes. He stood on his feet ten hours each night in the bakery that bore his name and brought home the platitudes of handwork. "Idle hands make mischief," he said, and one Friday evening, to keep me occupied, he showed me how to roll sandwich buns. We had time while my mother sliced apples for coffee cakes before she left him behind at the bakery at seven o'clock for the weekend's twelve-hour shift.

My father cupped pieces of dough. He rolled them in small circles, creating spheres and cupping the next pair as if he was teaching the secrets of the shell game my cousin Tim had fooled me with for ten nickels I'd taken from the change my mother kept in a jar on her dresser. I set fresh bits beneath my hands and pressed my way to embarrassment, rolling one lopsided ball and a thing that suggested turd. As if one side of my body was crippled, I couldn't make two circles at once, the left hand refusing the way it had begun to do for basketball and piano practices.

"Your Uncle Teddy had the same trouble way back when," my father said. His hands cupped and circled, cupped and circled without one word of advice about the way to bloom sandwich buns for families who were willing to pay for his hand-work. My mother set a bowl of sliced apples on the work bench and told me to wash my hands before I dragged filth into our car. "In a couple of years, he can help out here," my father said to her, but already I was beginning to tell myself a story about how useless my hands were, and I felt failure fill my throat like a comma while I paused and chose a future that relied on something other than how well I could use my hands.

The Privacy of the Hands

The next summer I believed a hillside of trees behind the houses across the street meant we'd moved close to where the rich lived, that our new house meant a baker could earn money like a lawyer or a doctor. I was about to enter junior high school, where the road to college began like it had for Tim, already a freshman there, who said, when he visited with Aunt Rhonda and his older sister Barbara, an eight-grader, that the two of us should go upstairs and jerk off while we talked about fucking her.

"You like looking at her, don't you?" he said, rubbing himself as soon as we were in my room. "You want your hands all over her naked body, right?"

He grabbed me between my legs and squeezed. "You're not even hard," he said. I was soft and small, suddenly knowing how skinny I was, how weak, that he could strangle me with his hands if that's what gave him pleasure.

"There's nothing in the whole world that feels as good as a pussy," he said, and he pulled my pants down and told me to play with my penis while he talked about all the parts of Barbara that he wanted to abuse until I got hard. "There," he said at last. When my hand slipped away, he stroked himself, crooning, "Do yourself, do yourself," and I came as soon as I followed his orders.

Arranging the Hands for God

My confirmation class, seventh graders, learned the perfect position to receive the body of Christ, kneeling to lay one hand open upon the other when we were asked to be supplicants. We learned the proper way to reach for wine, letting the blood of Christ be passed down to our half-raised hands from the minister's tray of tiny cups.

By now I knew that none of the fathers on our street had gone to college. "Why do you think lawyers and doctors would live in houses like the ones on our street?" my mother had said after we lived there for a month, and each Sunday, Communion sounded like pity on the part of God, some charity approaching us with its patronizing sack of coins. That winter, the minister changed his technique and laid the wafers directly on our tongues. My hands, unoccupied, gripped each other and waited for wine to be sipped from the common cup wiped dry after each upturned mouth had touched it.

All of us were infants at the rail, our hands used only for balance as we rose, steadying ourselves, returning to the hardwood pews where we sat in silence like Christian families were expected to, ready to sing the recessional hymn, four verses releasing us into weather that waited outside, regardless of communion and prayer, our fathers retrieving their cars like valets, their wives and children relaxing in the doorways like the wealthy.

The Whole World in my Hands

Week after week "He's Got the Whole World in his Hands" was Number One on the living room radio. For once, my father sang along with a popular song because Laurie London, the singer, meant we were all being watched over by a benevolent God.

I was glad He wasn't, because I didn't want anyone knowing that before sleep each night my hands loved the brief pleasure they made as I remembered the beautiful parts of girls from my invisible place in their lives. I stiffened and swelled as I imagined girls who would shudder and cry out and not care one bit about whether or not God was watching.

For a month, two other boys from my street and I played a board game that let us become owners of the whole world, in part, and then in bigger parts if we outsmarted each other, clever enough to consolidate our power like an army. When Tim visited, we played strip poker instead, and when one of those neighbors lost, going completely naked, Tim made him walk across the basement like he was a model.

In history class, during our six days with myths, Atlas held the whole world in place, using his legs and back, looking unhappy in his work, so much like a man underappreciated by his boss. My history teacher declared that the whole world was growing smaller, the globe shriveling from the cold of technology until it would fit in the soft palms of the wealthy.

Aunt Rhonda remarried. "A drinker," my mother said. "A big mistake." Aunt Rhonda stopped visiting, Tim turning into somebody I only saw at the family reunion we had at North Park every July. Where I wasn't kept expanding. The world lived in neighborhoods impossible to reach, so far away I wasn't even a story they heard about, let alone remembered.

At last the world I lived in chilled and contracted to something so small I thought I could carry it like a pen, one hand free to fend off the future's danger, what was coming no matter how much I learned.

Covering the Hands

Going to church meant my mother, like a surgeon, slipped on white gloves at the door. They said she was ready, and it was time for me to get in the station wagon, sit in back, and remember to keep the window rolled up. She held a tissue to the handles and knobs between our house and our pew. She wore them once and washed them; she owned a second, identical pair, three ridges along the back that matched the two pair in boxes she would save for Easter or Christmas or weddings that requested extended hands.

"White gloves," she said, "are like glasses," what she needed to see past herself. She wore them like lipstick, her hands bleached by etiquette. She prayed with her fingers gloved; she held the hymnal as if it were ice. The pairs that waited in boxes were like the souls of the unborn.

The Hand Jive

The summer before ninth grade I bought "Willie and the Hand Jive," by Johnny Otis, who sang that everybody could do that crazy hand jive. Roseanne Mort, who lived next door, could do the hand jive, and so could her friend Diane, both of them a year older like my cousin Barbara. They went to a Catholic school where they wore white blouses and plaid skirts every day until summer, when they sunbathed in two-piece swimsuits and I watched them from my upstairs window exactly the way Tim had told me I would.

One afternoon I took my shirt off and put "Willie and the Hand Jive" on my suitcase-sized record player and bounced a tennis ball off the back of our garage, pretending I was too busy to make the motions, their hands moving to the music while they lay on their backs in the sun. Their hands went still when the song ended. Neither of them looked my way.

The Importance of Hand Size

During the first social studies class I had in ninth grade, Mr. Martin had us all stand up. "As a welcoming present," he said, "I'm going to tell you who's going to be tallest when you're done growing."

I looked at Paul Hoak, who sat two seats behind me because Hoak followed Fowler in the alphabet. He was taller than anyone else in ninth grade, group A history and geography. "It's not just who's tallest now," Mr. Martin said, walking right up to Paul Hoak as if he knew what everybody was thinking. He had a tape measure and ran it from Paul's knees to the floor.

Paul Hoak didn't sit down after he was measured. He watched while Mr. Martin measured me and repeated the same number he'd said aloud for Paul. George Ware and Dwight Wiley, a few minutes later, had a number one digit higher than Paul and I. "There's your biggest guys," Mr. Martin said. "Just you wait and see."

"What about the girls?" Nancy Watkinson said. "Can't we be taller?"

Mr. Martin hesitated. "None of the girls will be that tall," he said, but Nancy stepped to the front of the room and stood up straight. Mr. Martin held the tape measure a foot from her knees, but she moved closer until it touched her. Her legs were thin and white; her knees were bare. When Mr. Martin read her number off the tape, she smiled. "I'll be taller than half the boys in this room," she said.

On the way home on the bus, Paul Hoak told me the size of hands was the way to predict something that mattered. He put his palm against mine, and his fingertips extended a quarter inch farther. "Get a load of that," he said. "My dick is bigger than yours, for sure."

"How's that work?" I said.

"The bigger the hand, the bigger the dick. Everybody knows that."

The Huns of Time

There's no escaping the Huns of Time is what I thought Aunt Rhonda's new husband said at the family reunion. He had badly fitted false teeth and an accent that slurred what he was saying until it was as hard to make out as Uncle Teddy's words after he was given a mechanical voice box. "The Huns of Time," he said, waving his beer can, "are never satisfied. There's no reasoning with them," intending, I thought, to make me see the way the Huns had invaded him.

They'd sacked Rome, I knew, come from someplace like Germany where my grandfathers had been born, speaking a dark language of coughs and growls. Some afternoons, when I was doing nothing but slouch in front of our small television, I thought I could hear the Huns of Time muttering among themselves outside.

Some nights, when the Huns slipped into the house, I could tell they'd quit high school like my cousin Tim, that they moved a lot because they couldn't hold jobs. Always, though, the Huns were having fun like Aunt Rhonda and her new husband, more of it, at least, than parents like mine who were punctual as dawn.

When I followed Tim and his two new brothers to the overlook near the picnic grove, he said he'd bet any money I still fucked my hands, and they laughed like the Huns who stuffed turkey legs in their mouths before they swallowed wine and beer in gulps. No wonder the Huns looked as happy as Tim. Their families were sure to join them, coming from over the horizon where they pillaged like darkness or light.

Soft Hands

After open house, after my father met Mr. Chase, my new social studies teacher, we walked outside before he shook his head. "Did you ever take notice of that fellow's hands?" my father said.

"Not really."

"You should learn to look where it's important," he said. "That man's hands are so soft you can tell he's never done a day's work in his life."

"Teaching's work."

My father acted as if he didn't hear me. He unlocked the car on the passenger side as if I was my mother. "You don't have tough hands, you don't have anything," he said.

I knew there wasn't a callus on my hands. For a moment, I

thought my father was going to grab my arms and turn my palms up for inspection, but he walked around to the driver's side without saying another word.

The next day I went into the garage and inspected his tools---shears, rake, hoe, pick, and shovel. I'd never touched any of them but the lawnmower. I carried the shovel across the street, between two houses, and down the hill into the woods.

I chose a spot that was nearly surrounded by trees and began to dig, telling myself I could do this for an hour every day until my hands would pass my father's test. After five minutes, I was sweating. After ten minutes, I was struggling with roots and stones. After half an hour, my hands showed blisters that I told myself were the necessary first step to calluses. "Ok," I said out loud. "That's a start," but the next afternoon I didn't go back with the shovel.

Wash Hands after Using

Though everyone knew you had to go upstairs for hot water, *Wash hands after using* was taped above the rust-stained sink beside the terrible basement toilet in my father's bakery. Nearly fifteen years-old, I knew bacteria could close businesses like my father's. They hid inside the near future like the stark, rogue cells of failure.

Just before closing, my mother scrubbed pans while steam spread around her like heaven's immaculate floor. When it vanished, my shift began its long high arc toward midnight while I handled tomorrow's food and waited on men who believed, leaving bars, they needed doughnuts or cookies, entire cakes and pies, each of those drunks sending me back to the sink where I scrubbed because my father made it clear that the hands that touched coins were tainted, that the hands that touched others were stained.

Some nights, there were women who laughed, leaning across the glass counter, their loose blouses falling open as if they were luring my hands to their breasts. Seeing them drove me downstairs for a few minutes of fantasy that demanded another scalding to keep from spreading whatever was carried by desire, finishing the things I owed my father just before my mother returned to drive my soft hands home dirty for sleep, giving the secret sins that wanted to kill me ten hours to plot while I slept until near noon, waking to lunch without washing, holding a thick, pressed meat sandwich, stuffing it down my throat with my filthy, soiled fingers because now I wasn't working for anybody but myself.

Holding Hands

During the freshman/sophomore dance, Mr. Chase paired boys and girls to do The Stroll. Nobody had to hold hands with someone they didn't want to touch, but I was paired with Nancy Watkinson, and I did my best to look cool beside her as we slid and turned our way between the lines of sidestepping classmates.

When the song ended, Nancy Watkinson took my hand as a slow song began. "I'm tired of standing around," she said. Nancy Watkinson let me guide her around the gym floor, our hands together. We swayed for two minutes while Frankie Avalon sang "Hey, Venus," sliding among the other dancers, and just before it ended, she put her face into my shoulder.

Nancy didn't look up when I leaned away from her, but even though the next song was slow, she backed away because my feet didn't move. She held my hands up in front of her face. "You have such small hands," she said. "Mine are almost the same size."

She smiled, and I clutched her body against mine, running my hands over the whole world of her clothed back until she said, her face against my shoulder, "What do you think you're doing?"

Tim's Hand

At our family reunion in the county park, Aunt Rhonda and her new husband Albert brought vodka in a frosted bottle and a half gallon of orange juice. My cousin Tim's new brothers didn't come. "They have a mind of their own," Aunt Rhonda said.

Albert clicked his glass against hers and said, "I'll drink to that," but all the other adults at the six picnic tables acted like they were happy to stick to beer or soda.

I didn't wait to see if Albert made another drink for Aunt Rhonda. All the soda I'd been drinking sent me to the park's nearest outhouse for the second time since I'd finished two burgers and a hot dog. When I was leaving the side of the outhouse marked Boys/Men, Tim grabbed me by the arm and held up two sections of pipe for me to see. "Pretty cool, huh?" he said. I was fourteen and he was sixteen, so I waited for him to decide whether he would make fun of me for not knowing why two pieces of pipe were cool. "You can make any kind of bomb you want if you know how," he said.

I stared at the pipes. They reminded me of sinks and toilets, but I didn't say anything. "You afraid to blow up the outhouse?" Tim said. "Is my little cousin a pussy?"

"What's it do?" I said. "You know. How much does it wreck?"

"It'll wreck your old man and Albert both if they're taking a crap beside each other. It'll send shrapnel right up their asses like a big hard dick."

I nodded like I thought that was something Tim's pipes might do, but I was guessing they would sound, if he was lucky, as loud as a cherry bomb. "You a pussy or not?" Tim said, pushing one of the pipes at me.

He was ready, I thought, to call me something worse and smack me like he always did at every summer reunion and Christmas visit, so I said, "Ok, I'll do the girls' side," figuring this would at least be a way to take a close look at whatever secrets I might learn from sneaking inside.

While Tim hissed "pussy" in my ear, I waited a minute to be sure nobody was taking her time in there. And then it was easy enough to stick the pipe bomb inside the door, not even inspecting the place like I planned on, the pipe not near anything at all but the wall because Tim had backed away and wasn't looking over my shoulder. I lit the fuse and ran to where he was waving from behind a set of swings.

It made a noise loud enough to get a crowd of relatives running over to the bathrooms. I stood beside Tim, looking casual, and then he said, "I'll stick mine in the boys' sink while everybody's looking in the other side. "They're so close now, it'll scare the shit out of them."

Tim opened the outhouse door and whispered, "Any pussies in here?" He smiled and looked back at me as I retreated to the swings. He stood in that open doorway just like I had and struck a match. When he lit the fuse, the pipe blew up in his hand, Tim screaming so loud I held the swing's chains tight in my hands and counted to ten before I jumped off and ran over like somebody who had no idea what had happened.

I reached Tim right after his step dad Albert came around the corner from the girls' side. Albert didn't even look at me, I got an eyeful of the empty space at the end of Tim's palm, the way the bones, uncovered where a thumb and an index finger should be, nearly glowed. The more I stared, the more of Tim disappeared. While Aunt Rhonda screamed, I thought that Tim would be gone if I watched for another minute, that there was no way he would ever punch me again or even call me names.

And then I thought that the world wasn't as simple as that. It was more complicated, something worse.

Mothering

1

The morning after, the Sunday newspaper calls me "a friend who stopped by to check on the recent stroke victim." Not the half of it, not even ten per cent, leaving out nearly everything that put me in those still-anonymous shoes.

So, listen. By 10 a.m. Saturday, after Linda Warren didn't answer when I called at 9 and then again at 9:30, I was dressed and out the door. Since her husband Hank's stroke going on six weeks ago, she'd never not answered my morning call. There was the chance she hadn't heard the landline because she was busy in the bathroom with Hank or herself. She could have been running late with her schedule because she'd had a hard time getting Hank put together, the muscles on his right side so clumsy now he couldn't button a shirt or tie his shoes, but I wanted to be sure this wasn't something more. It's never a good thing, frustration.

By then it was sunny and fixing to be the best early April weather of the year. Nice enough, anyway, for me to think about a long walk after I'd made my stop, locking my door and bringing along my key ring where I'd added the one for the Warren's front door after Linda had given it to me in the middle of February. So I could come and go at their place. So I could help with things after Hank had what she kept calling his "incident." And I walked slowly, giving the two of them another minute's time to be ready to welcome me.

Still, there wasn't an answer when I knocked and then rang the bell. Which is what the key was for. Which is how I walked in on such a thing that can best be described as "never in a million years," though not the half of that either, not by a long shot.

2

Monday doesn't ask me for anything more than the weekends do these days, but when it comes, I haven't been out of the house since I'd let myself into the Warrens, seen what I'd seen, and said my piece to the police.

By the looks of the newspaper, neither have any reporters. What's new according to them? Hank Warren is still unresponsive, in critical condition at the county hospital, but the doctors aren't releasing additional details. The police still have a person of interest for the crime, but they're not commenting further. Both of those items could have been had for one-minute phone calls, and for sure, there's no sign that someone might have persisted past "fine, let us know when you're ready."

One good thing about that—my name's not public yet, though maybe it's worse waiting for it to be shouted from half the front porches in the county at six a.m., my small role in a story where everybody, before they read any further, knows what will happen. It's like the way I remember reading Shakespeare fifty years ago, knowing all those people with their names in the titles, no matter how much they talk and talk in pretty language, are very shortly going to be dead.

3

Since Hank and I had retired five years ago, whether Thursdays were hot or cold or in between, Linda always made iced tea for after our dollar-a-stroke golf or during our nickel-a-point gin rummy, and then she busied herself someplace else in the house. "Big time gamblers," she said. She always had a book to read. A new one every time I stopped by. Even the thick ones were over and done with by the next week. "You two have your stories. I have mine."

Hank and Linda had lasted longer in marriage than me and my two wives put together. I'd managed twelve and eighteen years, and they were going on forty-five. "Hank's my best friend," Linda would say. "I've been lucky."

They'd never had kids, so there wasn't even that cliché of staying together for the children to fall back on as reason. Sometimes I thought them lasting was more surprising than most of the childhood-traumas-as-sources-of-issues I heard from troubled students from my working years, but then I'm not being a counselor when I think on marriage.

Hank was the one who labeled my work as mind-massages for the masses. He picked at my stories the way sports fans second-guess coaches. To tell the truth, I loved egging him on. Two weeks after his stroke, when I finally half-relaxed around him, I mentioned a student who had sued her college because it failed to account for her allergies to escalators, tall people and cactus. I wanted Hank to laugh and maybe forget himself for a few minutes. This student hadn't attended the college where I worked. Both of us were free to joke about something that seemed to make satire out of my job. "She'd be safe in here," I added, encouraging him by pointing out how he and Linda were short and didn't own a cactus or have an escalator in their small, one-story, two-bedroom house.

Hank didn't smile. "My mother always made me retie my shoes before she'd let me step onto an escalator," he said. "She told me never talk to big people I didn't know. Those aren't allergies. Those are fears. If you pay attention to that drivel, you'll spend your whole life making the weak feel important."

"What about cactus?" I said.

"That's just common sense." He looked at me as if he expected me to apologize for gullibility, but then he went on. "There wasn't any of that overthinking in driver's ed. Kids wouldn't last a day on the road thinking like that."

"Allergic to bridges," I said. "There's some drivers that are."

"They can walk then."

"Or live in Kansas."

"A clear head," Hank said. "Anticipation. A lot of what used to be called horse sense."

"Sounds right," I tried, but Hank seemed pensive.

"You have your pine trees and grass seed" he said. "Maybe you ought to sue the golf course for your lousy scores."

"There's medicine."

"For goddamned sure. I'm stuffed to the gills with it, but none of it says 'right-side hemiparesis.'"

"Lucky us," I said, meaning it, but Hank looked bothered, his eyes fixed on the carpet by Linda's empty chair as if he'd spotted crumbs from the oatmeal-raisin, vanilla, or anise cookies she baked every week to put out for us.

4

The story is still front page on Tuesday, but now there are two columns embellished with human interest, Hank and Linda's neighbors talking, their pictures to the side. All three neighbors say the same thing. Such a shock. A devoted couple. Linda the nicest person you could run into when you stopped in on business at the borough office. Linda so devoted to her job as secretary she never once complained about having to attend all those public meetings that dragged on forever because townspeople thought they had something that needed listening to. Linda, according to one, a possessor of a good soul whose anise cookies at Christmas and Easter not only were decorated with Christian images but tasted as if they were baked in heaven.

Hank, I thought, would agree with that in a slanted sort of way. "Arguing with Linda," he'd told me two weeks ago, "is like arguing with Jesus. All you earn is shame."

He had fans as well. "The sweetest little man" is how one of Hank's former driver's ed. students describes him. "So gentle." She's my daughter Kelyn's age, thirty-five, but I don't remember her being in our house. She's shown standing with three little kids and a baby in her arms, and I wonder whether her husband is as out of the picture as my Kelyn's. The yard around her house, I notice, has the same well-kept look as Hank's and Linda's.

I'd say we live in a neighborhood where violence is as rare as a tornado or a Democrat elected to office. The paper says the last murder in the borough was twenty-four years ago, a two-year-old child, and I remember at once how a young father had thrown his boy against the wall of his apartment. "Because he cried and cried and wouldn't stop," the baby-tosser had said.

Hank's condition is still described as critical. What's included, just after, are two sentences that name me as the frequent visitor who discovered Linda's dead body and Hank's unresponsive one. I lay the paper down on the kitchen table, put on a coat, and drop my keys in the pocket. I don't want to be home when the phone starts ringing, not even at 6:30 when some I know might call.

It's still half dark, so when I pause a few steps from the crime scene tape that's still up and intact, I finger the key Linda had given me, nearly pull it and the others from my pocket before I push myself down the block to keep from playing the fool.

By seven o'clock the sun has broken through, the morning brightening so intensely I start to think I'm being watched from houses where people live who recognize me. I imagine being stopped at the end of a driveway, a small crowd gathering to ask and ask. I take the shortest route back home, one that doesn't go past the Warren's house.

Two messages are blinking on the phone, and when it rings for the twentieth time before noon, I lock the door and drive off to see a movie. Tuesday afternoon, the one o'clock showing of 10 Cloverfield Lane has three other customers, each of us alone, each sitting in a center seat at least four rows apart.

All along I think John Goodman's character is right to be hunkered down in his bomb shelter because the aliens have arrived. Not because it makes sense to believe him, but because I'd seen the earlier Cloverfield movie, the one filmed with a hand-held camera so I felt like I was right there, where it felt real because things turned out badly. Walking out, though, I wish I had Hank Warren to tell that Goodman acted "movie paranoid," not much at all like my troubled students, who mostly stayed inside themselves the way I'd learned to do around my daughter since she'd turned overbearing after I'd retired, equating that natural event with senility.

I brought up one of those students to Hank about three weeks ago, a case more than seven years old so when I changed the boy's name and considered the time that had passed, I decided confidentiality had expired like my old income tax records.

The referral, I told Hank, had been made in person to me and my colleague Rachel Faust by a professor. He'd never heard or seen anyone picking on this student, he'd said, but the boy had begun to send him email messages claiming persecution and humiliation, saying how much he hated everyone, including him, for allowing it.

"The first time," the professor said, "I answered by email and suggested we talk, but he didn't show. The second time, I asked him to stay after class, but he walked right out. The third time I came to see you because I find myself watching his hands when he enters the room. I pay attention when he reaches into his backpack until he extricates a book or a notebook. Even worse, he always sits directly to my left so I have trouble keeping him in sight. I'd be dead in a heartbeat if he wanted it that way."

We did our jobs, I told Hank. We talked the student through the "situation," and Rachel set up weekly meetings with him after he seemed more at ease with a woman than with me. For a while, Rachel reported "promising progress." A few weeks later, though, that boy walked out of class and into the bathroom just across the hall so everyone in the class could hear him slam the walls with his fists and yell, "You fucking pussy" over and over, as if, the professor said later, he was admonishing himself for not shooting me and whichever students he held a grudge against.

Hank's expression didn't change. "Another professor brought the boy to the counseling center that day," I said. "He was teaching in an adjoining room and hurried to the door, which turned out to be unlocked. He led the boy outside and walked him straight to Rachel Faust."

By then Linda had shown up with two big tumblers of Arnold Palmers, what she'd started making after Hank's stroke, diluting the tea with lemonade to cut down on Hank's caffeine. Hank didn't reach for his, and Linda waited while I sipped and said, "Good batch."

A moment passed. Linda hovered. Hank stayed quiet in a way my mother used to call "down in the dumps." Like nothing could rouse him.

Linda glanced my way. "How's your girl getting along these days?" she said, and Hank sat up like he'd heard a cue from a prompter.

"That daughter of yours was a humdinger," he said.

The word sounded so suggestive I didn't know how to answer. Finally, Linda chimed in, "Whatever do you mean by that, Henry Warren?"

Hank smiled at me. "What? She never acted up around you?

Speaking her mind?"

Linda shook her head and disappeared into the kitchen; I said, "She's feisty."

"A humdinger. She had herself more spirit than brains when she first got behind the wheel. A heavy foot. Like a boy almost, how she went at it."

"She's always been her own self."

"That's another way of putting it," Hank said, and we both went silent for a few beats too long. The year before, Hank had asked three months running about my daughter right up until her divorce became final. "I kept hoping for some gumption from that man of hers," he'd said when I gave him the news.

"She says it's for the best," I'd said, and Hank shook his head as if he was disappointed by the final episode of a thirteen-week mini-series.

Linda, when I'd told her about the settlement, said "She needs a shoulder," and I imagined a much younger Linda baking and coddling for a few weeks while some boyfriend showed himself more and more to be a prick.

Hank turned animated, like his old self that would be ready to play a round of golf in forty-degree weather just because the calendar said Spring. "I bet you counseled some of my young drivers over the years," he said.

"Not that many townies attend, so maybe not," I said, but Hank didn't slow down.

"Or maybe you're doing right by them, keeping mum."

"Maybe."

"I'm here to tell you I remember them when I read about their crashes and their DUIs. How they acted at the start. How you could set your watch to inevitable. You do that with yours?"

"Mine scatter."

"So you never know the sheep from the goats?"

"Not often."

Hank lifted his glass left-handed, took a sip from his drink, and frowned. He put the glass down carefully, but it nearly tipped, some of the amber liquid splashing onto the table. "Fuck's sake," he muttered, glancing toward the kitchen, and he turned toward me.

"Those kids all expect something they'll never get, every last one of them, so you'll never be surprised."

Right then it was a relief to have Linda come back in with a plate of her Easter season anise cookies that meant she was joining us, that an hour had passed, maybe more, so she could spare a few minutes for small talk before I left. "Here's your favorites," she said, giving me one and placing one beside Hank's barely touched Arnold Palmer. She sat in her chair that was always protected with a shawl she'd bought years ago from an Amish woman who sold along the highway south of town.

"You hear how she has the hospice in her voice now?" Hank said.

Linda looked stricken, but Hank kept on. "She likes me being laid up. Like it's good for me to be dependent."

My cookie, I noticed, had two lilies embossed on its surface. There were crosses, doves and the face of Jesus on the others. I sat there deciding what I could say so that Linda wouldn't speak. As it turned out, a moment too long. "A little time off never hurt anybody," she said, biting into a cookie.

Hank pushed his cookie away from his glass until it looked as if it was meant for somebody who was expected to join us. "Hear that?" he said. "That's the speech you get after your nurse decides she knows your time's up." He lifted his glass and moved it beside the uneaten cookie. "Arnold Palmer should be ashamed of himself having his name on this kids' stuff."

"Now, now, Hank, you know why," Linda said.

"See?" Hank said. "See what I mean?"

On the phone the following morning, Linda volunteered, "He's not as bad off as he thinks he is." I could hear the television turned up loud coming from the living room where, by the sound of the dialogue, Hank was watching an old movie on the Turner network, sitting, I was sure, in his tan lazy-boy. "He can walk and talk and all that. Just slower with everything is all. I keep telling him he's seeing just a yellow light. Caution. You need some of that when you're seventy, stroke or no stroke, but he's already slammed on his brakes."

"A stale yellow," I said, but I heard Hank hollering from the living room, and Linda managed just "Excuse me" before she hung up.

5

I sleep in on Wednesday, the bleak weather keeping the light from the bedroom. When I rouse myself, I leave the newspaper lie outside in its rainy-day plastic wrap until I finish a cup of coffee. Which is why I don't get up from the dining room table while the phone rings at 8:45, figuring it's one of the twelve who left messages the day before. But when the voice mail kicks in, it's Kelyn leaving a message from two hundred miles away to tell me she's coming to visit to make sure I'm ok.

"Why wouldn't I be ok?" I try, picking up, and she's off and running. "Word gets around fast, Dad," she says. "Yesterday I got seven text messages saying you walked in on a murder scene."

"You don't have to come," I say. "I'm fine."

"It's no problem."

"I don't need anything," I say. "Stay home."

Though I'm sure it's moot, I hang up and manage a six count before the phone sounds again. She drops right back into her second-hand news. "This morning I got five texts that said it was your friend Hank Warren who's the murderer," she says. "I thought you said he had a stroke and lost most of his right side," letting me know what to expect in the plastic-protected newspaper before I retrieve it. "I'll be there tomorrow night. I'll leave the girls with my friend who loves to have them, no questions asked."

"I have questions," I say, but the line is already dead, nothing to do but pick up a little to keep her from starting a lecture. I empty two shopping bags of boxes Kelyn had brought as "a cheer-up present" the last time she'd visited. Altogether, there are two full outfits: a new shirt, a pair of pants, a sweater, even a warm-up suit and what any sensible person would know was nothing but an extra pair of tennis shoes. Before she'd left, she'd filled two plastic bags with old clothes of mine and said she'd help out by dropping them off at the Goodwill bin on her way out of town.

The story's been moved to the Local section, a good thing, because the first half of the front section has been dampened by water leaking under the plastic wrap. No matter what people were thinking before, now they know this was not a home invasion. Hank is the "person of interest," the sole suspect. There is a picture of Linda, a recent one, because she's wearing the glasses with the new frames she bought in January. Hank, it says, stands accused of bludgeoning his wife to death, beating her multiple times with a hammer found at the scene along with two empty vials of prescription drugs.

There's no sign of a neighbor or old student talking nice in this article. There's no sign of me except my name repeated in a cut-and-paste paragraph, nobody, not yet, interviewing me so I could tell them there are situations where you find out how many ways the world sticks to you. Seeing's just a part of it. Hank's clothes covered in blood. Linda's body on the living room floor nearly hidden under a blanket. There's silence, too, Hank so still slumped in his lazy-boy that I leaned down to feel for a heartbeat in his throat warm to the touch and faintly pulsing. Smell? Blood soaked into the carpet, the worst.

And the glass of white wine by the kitchen sink, nearly full, and me, without thinking, picking it up and sipping before I dumped it down the drain and ran water over it and set it back to dry, thinking, right then, that I'd walked in on something absolutely and purely inexplicable. Unless Hank Warren survives to tell his tale. Unless he beats the odds of tragedy.

6

Two Thursdays before the murder, as I told Hank about another seven-year-old case, he seemed to perk up. I took it as a signal to elaborate on a student who, despite having been hauled into the student life office for multiple offenses, proved to be friendly when he came in to talk. With his phone, he'd secretly taken pictures of his resident assistant and a few other students who lived in his hall and posted them on Facebook with the headings "asshole" and "douchebag" and "dickface." When some other students "liked" and even
shared those pictures, it became fan-club-like, something more than nuisance when it tuned out he'd also made crude drawings on notebook paper of those students, each identified by name in a caption below their bodies being stabbed and bleeding.

The boy, I said, had left the pictures sit in plain sight on his dorm room bed long enough to be discovered by the resident assistant, which is when Hank interrupted. "That sneaky one from last week is the danger,"

Hank said. "The stabber artist is just showing off. He's a little wuss."

When I smiled, Hank snorted. "You and your ambition. You should have stayed in the high school where people know what needs to be done. The college left the sneaky prick stick around, didn't it? And dumped the kid who drew cartoons."

"Uh-huh. Before you could say "fantasy," it was a real mess. I did my best to mitigate the inevitable. I wrote a letter expressing my sense that this boy wasn't a threat."

"Not your call?"

"Rachel Faust's, but student life had already decided."

"A woman's going to vote against blood every time."

"What a counselor you'd make, using gender as the first criterion."

"If I was prejudiced, I wouldn't have passed any of the girls who never stopped talking while they were driving."

"I know one of them," I said, and for once, Hank laughed aloud and spouted the names of three students, all boys, he'd refused to have in his driver's ed. car. "One time only offenses," he said. "Talk about your dickheads, six years apart coming through, the three of them, but each was hopeless, so I said, 'Ask your fathers to teach you this one thing.' No doubt about it, those boys were always a danger to themselves, but in a car, they were a danger to others, so absolutely no more. Nobody complained or called the principal. Those fathers had to know exactly why I wouldn't have their sons in the car ever again."

Hank took a couple of quick breaths, panting like he'd just finished a dash down the block and back, before he settled in the lazy-boy and closed his eyes. I waited a minute, feeling like I was being tested, but though it had been nearly an hour, Linda didn't bring in the Arnold Palmers, so I made my way to the front door, turned to look back just to be sure, and found Linda coming into the foyer from the kitchen. "Good for you, letting him feel smart," she said.

"I didn't want to get him worked up."

"Thank you for that as well. I know he has his ways, everything either right or wrong. A boy's way of seeing never quite left him."

"Nuance isn't his friend," I said.

"That's why I'm so happy you've kept coming by every week since the incident. You're a prescription, and he doesn't even know it. He gets a dose with his tea and lemonade."

"Or without," I said, and she looked back into the living room.

"I'll make his tea straight again next week. Maybe normal's better even if it's pretend."

"Normal's what you make of it."

Linda stepped closer to me, nearly whispering. "You know what Hank has said at least once a week for thirty-five years every time he's angry over nothing? 'Driver's ed. is a fool's job.'"

"Everybody has doubts about what they do," I said, but she wasn't finished.

"Not like Hank when he got going. 'Anybody can drive,' he'd say. 'Just look around. It's easier to drive than to print your name. It's like the only math you need can be counted on your fingers.' Everybody said Hank was a great teacher, but I'm the one who knew all that time that he hated that nobody thought he was smart."

7

Today is the Thursday I was going to tell Hank Warren about the woman who was allergic to mauve. She claimed pale purple shortened her breath. It's warm enough Linda would have talked him into sitting outside on the screened-in porch, the only change they'd made in that house since they'd moved in when I was still working with Hank at the high school.

I thought it would be good for him to mock me for even mentioning that one with a straight face. But what I really wanted was a prelude to telling him and Linda about my daughter's allergy to gold, how the impossible can be fact.

The night Kelyn turned twenty-one, a friend at a bar bought her a special liqueur speckled with gold dust. As soon as she swallowed, her throat shut tight. She gasped and wheezed; her friend begged the bar for a doctor; strangers stared and did nothing until the seizure somehow passed.

"Like children watching a magician," I said when she told me, and she answered, "I could have died a metaphor, the woman with an allergy to gold" before we walked outside, the day clear, just before sunset, as if we needed to dare both the light and dark.

8

The last Thursday before the murder I told Hank that the dagger and blood boy became my Facebook friend. He doesn't post often, I told Hank, but a couple of years ago he posted himself and a girlfriend in caps and gowns graduating from another college. And when Facebook dropped in one of those You've Been Friends for Seven Year photos as compulsory nostalgia, it was the picture of me he'd posted right after I agreed to be his friend. I'm slouched in the school snack bar, and inexplicably close to me is a stuffed panda that belonged to his then-current girlfriend.

"There's a thing called play therapy," I told him. "Way back when we were kids, Life magazine had an article about it, a psychiatrist using a boy who heaved clay against the life-sized scrawled drawing of his brother, the body chalked on the wall like the dead. The patient declared he was happy now, and though not exactly in love with that hated brother, he'd stopped screaming, 'I want to kill you!'"

"See?" Hank said. "The know-it-alls were wrong."

"I message him from time to time like he's an outpatient," I said.

"All you have to do is wait for the other guy to snap," Hank said. "Then you can message your old friends from student life and give them a Facebook poke."

Linda walked past the doorway with a book, but she didn't say anything. Without the Arnold Palmers or the straight ice tea or the cookies, it felt as if I'd just arrived. Hank rapped on the arm of his chair like a teacher. "Listen," he said, "can you remember the time when you wanted your mother to stop touching you. You know. Fixing your collar or smoothing your hair."

"I guess there was a time," I said. "Maybe when I turned thirteen or something like that."

"I was ten," Hank said. "It was my birthday, and she kept fussing with my hair, taking her own comb to it like I was a simpleton. I had friends about to arrive, and she kept saying "birthday boy" like she'd never seen me before. As soon as the doorbell rang, I ran my hands through my hair so it fell all over the place before I answered."

9

When I open my door, Kelyn throws her arms around me, but I feel myself stay rigid for a second before I move one hand onto her back. "You poor thing," she says, "having to see all that and him your friend and such a nice, gentle guy." When she doesn't let go, I step back, and she says, "Are you ok?"

"You know what drivers ed. story Hank Warren told me just two weeks ago?" I say. "He wanted me to know that over the years he'd forced three boys out of the car and made them walk back to school."

"Everybody knew that story when I had him," Kelyn says, "but nobody knew what made him so angry."

"Something about putting others in danger, but what I think he meant was they wouldn't listen."

"All that tough guy stuff about making kids walk. It was like a myth, Dad. Like that woman in the Bible who turned to a pillar of salt for not obeying. He must have thought those stories made it easier to teach us."

"He said you were a humdinger. His word. It means you never shut up and drove too fast, too soon."

Kelyn smiled. "He really was sweet, Dad. We had to change a tire for a test. Everybody dreaded it. There was a boy in my group, a head, you know, a druggie kid, and when it started to rain really hard while he was right in the middle, you know, the tire off, but the other one sitting there, Mr. Warren got out and finished up for him."

"To be kind or because he had no patience?"

"I don't know, Dad. He's your friend."

"In that case, because he wanted you to see how competent he was."

"You mean another myth? Jesus, Dad, you talk as if you'll testify against him. Maybe they'll find out she had cancer or something. He covered her, Dad, and then he tried to kill himself with all that medicine."

"Who beats his wife with a hammer if it's a mercy killing/suicide?"

"He killed her with one blow and the others were just making sure. Or he thought he could kill her with one blow, but the stroke made him swing left-handed, and he had to keep going once he started. Don't you hope for that?"

"There's no reason to hope for the impossible."

Kelyn starts to stack the old newspapers and gathers one empty frozen dinner dish that sits on the coffee table. "Look at this place. You go relax and let me clean up for a while before I take you out for a decent meal." She runs water in the sink and squeezes detergent into it before dropping silverware and dishes into the soapy water. "I'll stay until Sunday, Dad. Help you catch up with things like laundry and shopping." I go and sit on the porch and wait for her to exhaust her charity.

When she comes out at last, the twilight starting to fade, she goes to her car and comes back, thankfully, with only her suitcase. "I'll take it inside later," she says, "and I'll make a grocery run after dinner."

For what? I want to say, but I begin to tell her what I know about Hank and Linda, how the police were waiting to get the full story because all this was such a surprise. "It sounds so open and shut," I say. "I keep thinking that all those clues won't let me see any way but straight in Hank's eyes. Hank's my friend, and yet I missed something beforehand."

"That's called normal, Dad."

"Normal's not enough then. I never even saw your Donny for who he was."

"Dad," Kelyn says, "Hank's not my story. Donny never touched me. He was just 24/7 needy. Mom called him the Wicked Witch of the West's little brother, a man who'd melt if somebody turned up the thermostat."

"And now here you are mothering like you have everything figured out."

"It's just housework, Dad."

"Unless a visitor does it. Then it's called patronizing."

"You want me to shut up?" she says. "How's this?" and she zips her lips together with one finger to make it clear she's done talking.

I give it a minute. Kelyn keeps her lips tight, but she doesn't turn away. "Your mother had a way with words," I say. "She told me I'd been a counselor so long I'd forgotten who people really were. She called it hand-holder's paradox—the more you try to help somebody, the less you know about them."

It sounds so weak, I look right at Kelyn and start again. "Your mother always hated Donny," I say. "From the very first. Maybe that's what made her so sure she knew everything about him, but I was always hoping you'd work it out."

Kelyn sighs, but her shoulders don't slump, and I feel a surge of panic. "For the girls," I say and hear my voice crack.

Kelyn turns, her gaze going out across the yard. There's nothing I can think of to do but turn as well, looking toward where the darkness amplifies how the forsythia's annual bright yellow is fading. In a few days, the bushes will be all green and nothing but a hedge-clipping job all the way to October. For a moment, I thought either I would ask her to leave or she would do it on her own accord.

"The thing is, Dad, I did work it out," she says.

I feel her hand on my arm, and I steady my eyes on the forsythia, allowing my fear and anger to pass. I want her hand to rest there, but it lifts as quickly as comfort.

The Variance

IN SEPTEMBER, WHEN HE TOLD HIS WIFE that his dentist had said, "You're never too old" as he showed him the x-ray that revealed his impacted wisdom tooth, she laughed.

"That sounds like a bedroom come-on," she said.

He didn't tell her he'd felt like hugging the dentist, overjoyed that the source of his jaw pain, at sixty-eight, wasn't something worse. Cancer, for instance. He'd been evaluating the odds, his jaw on fire. Nothing like a tooth ache. Deep in the bone. Ewing's sarcoma is what he'd self-diagnosed on Web MD. By then, his wife was a three-year survivor.

OVER SIX WEEKS NOW, since he's received a letter from the borough zoning board announcing that a variance is being sought by the Forward Company to erect a cell tower at the end of his street. One hundred twenty feet high, about the same distance, he guesses, from the potential tower site to the edge of the retired librarian's recently reseeded lawn, a little more than one hundred yards to where his property begins two doors down. Now that it's May, her grass is beginning to fill in around her rebuilt house, her entire lot, the one closest to the community pool, torn up after the fire leveled the old one last June. The variance, the letter says, follows the offer by the community pool to lease its land as a way to raise funds.

She had been retired two weeks when the fire struck. She's had it reconstructed exactly the same as it was, she's told him, cloned from photographs and blueprints that survived in a fireproof, padlocked box.

Three months after that fire, two weeks after his fiftieth high school class reunion, the ache he'd felt in his jaw since he'd driven home from Pittsburgh had exploded into pain.

HE WAS SCHEDULED FOR A PRE-OP CONSULTATION with an oral surgeon. In the waiting room, he'd read a set of sayings from dentists past that were listed on a poster: "A frog tied to the jaw can make teeth firm" was accredited to ancient Rome. "A live mouse held to the gums stops toothache" had been prescribed in Egypt.

Culture by culture, the long-ago dentists offered cures, and he followed the nostrums of the ignorant, admiring the strategy of placing such a poster in the waiting room, something to make patients believe they were lucky to be waiting for sophisticated technology and lengthy education to cure them. Just before the lowest item on the poster sank into shadow behind the bowed head of a woman who was waiting for her own oral correction was "Scratch painful gums with the teeth of a man who has died violently," but he could not see who was given credit for that prescription, not even when he rose, because his standing straightened her in her chair as if she thought he'd cut in line.

He'd joked with the oral surgeon about hoarding the world's oldest impacted wisdom tooth, fifty years since the others had been pulled, stitches sewn and removed, the next Saturday, by a dentist who died the following night.

The oral surgeon didn't change expression. He said, "We have to be cautious because of your age, but you look healthy." The surgeon didn't elaborate on what there was about his face and body to account for that diagnosis. He moved on. "I don't see many like this," he said. "Half a century, it's been lurking under there. You could say it's been in a blind spot all these years, and now you can hear it calling for help."

"Like some abused girl who's all grown up now and finally tells her story?"

The surgeon kept his eyes on the x-ray. "You could put it that way," he said, "but I wouldn't."

THE BOROUGH'S COMMUNITY ROOM HAD BEEN PACKED for the first open forum about the variance. The zoning board, after a few minutes, voted to grant the tower builders a six-week continuance. "After seeing all these people," the librarian had said, "Forward will have backup next time. They'll show up with lawyers and engineers."

This afternoon, from his front yard, he watches her house being filled with furniture. When she notices him, she points toward where the tower will thrust up next to the pool. When he answers with a hands-up shrug, she beckons him onto her front walk.

"I keep seeing that monstrosity standing right there in front of us forever," she says.

"Me, too," he says, but he doesn't see anything except the towers he passes when he is in a car, ones that are a hundred yards away or, most often, more. "Maybe you get used to it, having one close. Like all those phone poles and that maze of wires that passes overhead and you don't even see them after a while."

"Just take a walk into town. They're everywhere on the side streets near the river. You can't miss all that crap."

"See?" he says. "I never noticed."

"If you're trying to be ironic," she says, "it's not working."

He isn't, but he shuts up so she believes he is.

WHEN HIS WIFE WAS STILL IN REMISSION, when she came along to the oral surgeon to drive him home because, she told him, you're kidding yourself about doing that yourself, she'd brought along a <u>New Yorker</u> to read. The week before, after his consultation appointment, he'd told her <u>Field and Stream</u>, <u>People</u>, and <u>AARP</u> were the only magazines he'd seen, and she'd sighed. "Hunters, celebrities, and old people—you think he subscribes for his customers or himself?"

"The addresses are torn off from all the front covers. Maybe they're not his."

"Or maybe he knows his customers."

After the operation, she'd made him scrambled eggs and hash browns. "Soft and easy before the drugs wear off. You'll thank me."

And he had, at least, done that.

THAT FIRST VARIANCE LETTER HAD BEEN A LESSON about keeping watch over what you own. That tower would be so high and so close it might reach the librarian's house if it ever fell.

He wondered, too, whether the shadow of something that tall would reach his yard in late afternoon, a narrow darkness prying open his anger every sunny summer day at six o'clock.

Because it arrived on a Thursday and he waited until Saturday to go through his mail, he hadn't read that letter about the open hearing for two days. And then he'd gone up and down the street knocking on his neighbors' doors to poll them about the extent of their anger. Half way, he'd run into the librarian, who was already soliciting signatures for a petition to halt the company.

She followed him and sat in his living room for a few minutes. "We can't allow this to happen," she said. "I'm asking everyone to chip in for a lawyer. Someone who lives in town. Someone who gets it about keeping things the way they are."

When he asked her how her new house was coming along, she told him her story, how she'd taken her mother shopping and wasn't home when the fire started. How she thought, every day, about the excellent chance she would have noticed that fire early enough to keep the damage minimal. "At the very least," she said, "without my mother waiting upstairs by the front door, I would have taken the time to be more careful with the lint trap before I turned on the dryer and left for the mall."

AFTER HIS TOOTH WAS PULLED, the surgeon advised that he had some waiting to do in order for nature to take over and heal what he called "your wound." His wife cooked from a covered-dish menu of mac and cheese, baked beans, and spaghetti. She served him applesauce and ice cream. He dreamed about the steak dinner he was going to have after the surgeon pulled his stitches and gave him the thumbs up. On the sixth day, his wife came home from the grocery with a strip steak and a piece of halibut for herself. "Expensive," she said, "but let's celebrate."

The following morning, pain settled in so deep in his mouth that by the time he arrived for his appointment, he was in worse misery than before the extraction. He waved the dental assistant away, and the surgeon, when he took a look, said, "Looks like you've got something going on in there," an odd thing for a surgeon to offer when he was referencing his handiwork.

Infected is what he meant. Badly. But there were antibiotics to clear that up. His wife stowed the steak and fish in the freezer. "It will taste just as good regardless," she said. A week later, the surgeon removed the stitches, but two days after the antibiotics cycle expired, he was in pain. Another cycle, another antibiotic. Two days after the second cycle ended, the pain flared again. The surgeon took another x-ray. He described the third cycle as "aggressive." There was urgency in his voice. He floated the possibility of further surgery, operating on the bone itself.

A FEW DAYS BEFORE HIS WIFE'S HEADACHES RETURNED, he'd said, "It feels like he raped my mouth."

"Stop," she'd said.

"I'll stop when my jaw is safe. Right now, it has PTSD—every time I chew, it has flashbacks."

"I hope I'm the only one you talk to like this."

"I think worse, and then I censor myself before I tell you anything."

AT THE RESCHEDULED OPEN MEETING, the zoning board chair declares five minutes per speaker as the rule. The Forward Company, he says, will go first.

The company spokesperson says, "We're represented this evening by the firm of Hart and Mickley." The lawyer wears a suit that declares expensive and tailored. Across the aisle, the neighborhood lawyer wears a suit that looks like the two in his closet, one for summer, one for winter, both purchased years ago as preparation for weddings and funerals.

The spokesperson spends ten minutes introducing his list of speakers, filling in credentials that are weighted with accomplishments and awards. The engineer takes twelve minutes and apologizes when the overrun is noted. The site planner takes ten. Altogether, the four speakers go on for nearly an hour. The last to speak is a man who'd been a swimming pool originator nearly fifty years before. We need the money, he says, nearly sobbing. He tells stories of the origin and goes on nearly fifteen minutes without anyone stopping him.

The chair of the zoning board suggests a ten-minute break that lasts twenty. When the room regathers, half the chairs are empty.

"We need to keep the five-minute rule," he says. "Joelle, who's been busy keeping notes down at the end of the table, will hold up a yellow card when you reach four minutes and a red card when your time is up."

The first speaker announces there are already 820 signatures on a petition to block the cell phone tower. She holds up a sheaf of papers.

The lawyer rises and says, "Those have to be verified. They may or may not be legitimate. We need to examine them." He notices that the lawyer's hair is so perfect it looks as if it has been carefully trimmed during the break.

When the time comes for him to speak, he decides to say what his wife would have said. He stands and begins to speak about health issues connected to cell phone towers. "Especially vulnerable," he says, "are children. There is a school close by, and the pool is used primarily by children. There are studies that have shown . . ." Which is when the lawyer interrupts.

"Those studies have been disputed," the lawyer stands to say. "They have no bearing here."

"Nonetheless," he says, and hands the studies to the zoning board. When the lawyer approaches and demands they be discarded as inappropriate, the chair returns them.

The librarian follows him. She says she will read a letter she's written. It tells the story of her fire and her rebuilding. It explains how meticulous she has been in making sure everything is exactly as it was before, and now she feels as if lightning is about to strike her house and burn it down a second time.

Every member of the zoning board, he notices, is reading along with her, and he knows she has given each of them a copy beforehand. She goes on about being a thirty-year resident. That the street is immaculate and well-kept by every resident That it is unchanged.

Joelle holds up the yellow card, but the librarian doesn't speed up. She reads slowly and clearly about how the residents tolerate the traffic in summer because they, too, love the pool. Joelle holds up the red card and says "Time."

The librarian says, "Each of us on the street and the one just below us has pledged to make a donation to the pool." There is applause from the scattered townspeople who are left. He notices that two of the board members join in, that Joelle puts the red card down so she can clap. The librarian ends by looking directly at the company spokesperson: "I had my house rebuilt with no changes whatsoever. I hope to count on what's next door to remain unchanged as well."

JUST BEFORE HIS WIFE HAD EXPERIENCED what she called "a setback," he'd returned to his regular dentist to explain about the ache after he chewed, and worse, how his teeth didn't seem to meet on one side. "You know," the dentist said, "the x-rays that were sent to me after you called show your jaw's been cracked. Look. See there? I called your surgeon, but he disagreed."

"Cracked? You mean broken?"

"Yes. He should have told you."

"But not a word."

"You have reason to have an ongoing concern," the dentist said, "but I can at least build up those teeth and give you a better bite." He had his assistant schedule an appointment for the following week.

AT THE END OF THE MEETING, the lawyer announces the company is asking for a continuance, that it is now preparing a request for a variance because of providing "an essential service." He describes the dead spot on the road below where the pool is located, how travelers lose contact, how the tower will fix that disruption in communication. "And," he finishes, "as a gesture that recognizes community concerns, the Forward Company agrees to lower the proposed height of the tower to ninety feet."

BEFORE SHE'D GONE INTO THE HOSPITAL, his wife had pointed out how the librarian's house was beginning to reform the way their crepe myrtle had returned after it had died, flourishing from the base of the waist-high stump he'd left only because it was so difficult to saw and dig up.

Today, when he goes into the librarian's house, he sees that the living room has been arranged the same as it was before. The furniture appears to match what had been burned. The television looks as if it's the identical size. The chair her mother sits in is set in what he senses is the exact same spot.

"It's not a perfect match," the librarian says. "No matter how hard I tried."

"You have to look close the way you need to do to detect a quality counterfeit."

"No, not like that," she says. "Everything is real."

Her mother leans forward in her chair. The television volume slides up a bit, and he listens to a panel of women talking about the behavior of an actress.

The librarian moves two steps closer to her mother and stops as if there's a spot that's been blocked for her to speak from. "Mother," she says, and the volume decreases.

"I tried to call you earlier to say I wanted to stop by," he says. "You don't have an answering machine."

"Mother gets upset when she hears voices of people she doesn't know. Everybody I'm close to knows to call back."

"And no caller ID either?"

"Oh no. That computer voice would always be a stranger. She couldn't live with that."

"I want to try something about the dead spot. I want to make sure you're here to pick up. I'll drive up the hill through that stretch they're using as an excuse for providing an essential service to see if it's real. I've never called anyone from there because it's right on the other side of the hill so close to home."

"Sure," she says. "I'll pick up. I always do, no matter what."

At the red light at the base of the hill, he calls her number. She answers as the light changes. "Ok,' he says, "I want you to say, 'No cell phone tower' over and over and you can tell me how many times you said it—ready?

"No cell phone tower," she says. "No cell phone tower ..." and his phone goes dead,

It takes nine seconds for her voice to return. "How many times?" he says, and her absence, after he subtracts, is four. The math tells him the dead spot is barely more than a tenth of a mile, maybe 200 yards. Instead of going back to her house, he walks to the proposed cell tower site. Through a stand of trees, he can see the dead spot along the highway. The hillside is so steep, it is nearly all sheer rock.

WHEN HIS WIFE HAD BEEN HOSPITALIZED, he'd renewed her subscription to *The New Yorker,* a surprise he intended to show her when the expiration of the address label changed. Three weeks, it took, and by then she wasn't reading, her vision uncertain, her headaches insistent. He'd placed the issue with the updated subscription on top of the copy from the week before and done nothing but hold her hand. He'd carried both those issues home the following week and kept them and each succeeding one, looking, each week, at the cartoons, first covering the captions with one hand and creating one of his own, trying for a match.

THE DAY BEFORE HIS TEETH-CAPPING APPOINTMENT, the surgeon's receptionist had called to tell him the surgeon had closed his practice. "Just like that?" he'd said.

"Just like that," she said. "Consider yourself lucky. Your business here is over and done with. There's plenty in the middle of things who need attention."

"Why now?" he said.

"It's a personal matter," she said.

He'd waited. He'd taken three breaths.

"I've been told to ask everyone to respect the doctor's privacy," she said.

"Your records will arrive at your place of residence by registered mail."

"MISTAKES WERE MADE," the dentist had said, sounding eerily like Richard Nixon, but he had concentrated on the plural that had been used. The possibilities began to seem unlimited.

The dentist formed small caps from resin and sealed them to eight of his teeth so they could meet again on the left side of his mouth. "Old friends," the dentist said, and because he was grateful, he smiled an agreement and thought of returning to food untouched for months.

"Collateral damage," the dentist said, deflating the mood. "Your bite can be improved, but your jaw has been weakened. Aggressive chewing will likely bring a return of discomfort."

He said nothing, and the dentist soldiered on. "This will buy you a few years. Whoever replaces me when I retire later this year will know what to do when the time comes."

"Every dentist I know is retiring."

The dentist hesitated a moment before he said, "I'm surprised Charley has closed his practice. He's younger than I am by a decade."

"Me too," he'd said, and pushed himself out of the dental chair.

"One more thing," the dentist said. "This procedure is classified as cosmetic by Medicare. I'm sorry. Like all of us, Charley would have insurance to protect himself. Get in touch and see if they'll cover this."

"YOUR STORY'S MORE BELIEVABLE if you subtract something," the librarian said after he told her about his newly-capped teeth and broken jaw. "The way it is now, it sounds as if you're throwing everything in there but the kitchen sink."

"But it's true," he said. "As factual as your house burned to the ground."

"Now you sound like somebody who doesn't know the difference between a story and the truth."

The volume on the television soared. Her mother was watching the Food Channel. "Mother likes the chefs who don't use spicy things in their recipes," the librarian said.

HE OPENS HIS MAIL IMMEDIATELY NOW. When a letter quickly arrives from the surgeon's insurer regarding his damage claim, he learns that a decision has been delayed, although he should know it will be addressed thoroughly and fairly in all good time.

A WEEK LATER, the request for the variance is withdrawn. "The board didn't vote," the librarian says. "The company withdrew." She seems giddy. "I feel like Elliot Ness in The Untouchables. We couldn't get them legally for all the terrible things they were planning, but we got them on decency."

If his wife were alive she would tell him to appreciate his small, good fortune. That if he'd only look from the right angle, he'd see how lucky he was. When he always started with the worst scenario, didn't he notice that it was listed as least likely?

THE NEXT DAY the librarian tells him the Forward Company is going to put the tower up at the VFW. "It's a different zoning board over that way. More lax. Anybody can tell just looking at where it's located. It's only a quarter mile difference, but it's not right here in my face. Everything will be the same as ever."

THE POOL FILLS WITH TREATED WATER for the new summer season. The Saturday before Memorial Day, the gates open. Because there is no parking on his street, families climb paths rising steep from the high school lot. Some of his neighbors have invited their grandchildren, who all seem to be wearing new bathing suits as they walk past. In that morning's newspaper, there is a letter from a man who gives his address as "near the VFW." He describes the streets nearest to the pool as a small, desirable neighborhood, the people who live there as privileged as those who live behind attended gates.

IN THE MAIL, he receives a refusal from the surgeon's insurer. It explains that he signed a waiver before his surgery. He runs his tongue over the caps, conjuring the word "vulnerable." "It's not a lot of money," he thinks. "It's not serious damage." He gets in his car. Because there are parents dropping off teenagers and older children before turning around in the librarian's driveway, the street is swarming with cars.

FIVE MINUTES LATER, he calls the librarian as he approaches the highway's dead spot. "Hello," she says, and when he doesn't answer, she says, "Hello, who is …" before her voice disappears. Ten seconds later she is saying, "Please, who's calling?"

He turns around in the VFW parking lot, imagining the tower extending up from the corner of the lot. High enough, despite the distance, to be seen from his house. Even more visible from the librarian's house. Maybe, he thinks, the newest letter-writer will win with outrage, and the dead spot will be safe.

He doesn't call until he's looped all the way around and coming back up the hill. "Hello," the librarian says again, before her voice disappears. "Who is this?" she says ten seconds later, and he hangs up as he slows to make the left turn toward his house.

While he waits for an approaching car to pass, he looks in the rear-view mirror. The driver behind him pulls closer and taps his horn as soon as the car clears the intersection. A second, and then a third car pulls up behind.

Instead of turning, he presses redial and holds the phone to his ear. Listening to the librarian begin to plead, he counts to ten. The librarian stays on the line, but he can barely make out what she is saying because three horns are blaring in unison.

Dogs in Space

"THEY FIGURED OUT HOW to bring those dogs back from outer space," my father said. "The Communists. Their last two dogs are safe and sound. That means they'll have somebody in space any day now. Just you wait."

I didn't care about dogs in space. My father, fifteen minutes earlier, had announced we were moving, right after New Year's Day, to upstate New York so I would have to get used to the idea of finishing ninth grade in a new school. Now he was changing the subject before my older sister came home and he had another angry kid to deal with. "Now's not the time for rockets and such," my mother said, and my father walked outside as if he had something important to do in the yard.

Even though my mother began by saying, "Your father's been promoted, you should be happy," my sister screamed when she told her he'd been transferred as part of the deal. She was about to be a junior, she said. Nobody moves to a new school when they're that old. For the next four months she tried, without success, to work out a way to live with a friend until she graduated. What I did was wish my father had kept our move a surprise because for all those months up to Christmas vacation I felt like I was a visitor at school, a foreign exchange student who was about to be forgotten by everybody who acted like a friend.

The next time my father mentioned the Russian space dogs was a week after we moved into our new house. There we were, all of us sitting at the kitchen table for a dinner of cold sandwiches because something was wrong with the stove the last owners had left behind, and he told us how disappointed he was that 1960 had ended and nobody was in orbit. "Not even another dog," he said. "The Russians must have run into trouble. Maybe it's too cold for the Commies to blast off. Maybe they have to wait until spring."

"If it's anything like it is here," my mother said, "they can't even drive to where the rocket is sitting. I've never seen so much snow."

"It's freezing here," my sister said. "There's snow piled up outside like we're in Siberia or something."

"They have lake effect storms here, Bonnie," my father said. "There's Lake Ontario almost right next door, and something that big water changes things. You'll get used to it."

After a week, I knew all about lake effect storms. The roads had been mostly clear when we'd moved in, but since then, we'd had two snow days, and even when we went back, the snow was piled up along the street as high as my head when I walked. "Thank the Lord for the sidewalk plow," my mother went on. "What a blessing that is."

"It's not the Lord who pays for that plow," my father said.

"YOUR MOTHER SAYS THAT SHAMBACH BOY was here again," my father said the following week. "He's a bad egg, that boy."

My mother fluttered near the sink, washing enough spinach to make our fourth hot dinner into something I wasn't looking forward to. "His father is the high school principal," she said.

My father studied the water running over the dark green leaves before he turned and faced me. "Then you're in for it," he said. "A man can't raise his son has no business inside a school."

I had to admit I didn't like Len Shambach much more than my father did, but right then I was happy to have one boy my age as a friend. He lived more than a mile outside of town, but both Saturdays since we'd settled in ten miles from Rochester his mother had dropped him off while she shopped and did whatever else took all afternoon to finish. I'd tried out late for the ninth-grade basketball team my first day, and Len had started right in talking like I'd been on the team since November.

That first Saturday he'd snapped the tip off one of the cue sticks my father had hung on the basement wall after someone from the nearby sporting goods store had put the pool table we'd moved with us back together again. Worse, Len had made tiny holes in the basement wall with darts. When I'd turned eight, my father had shown me how to use a cue stick properly and control a dart, but they were supposed to be off limits to my friends unless he gave them a lesson, and now there were two reasons for him to ban me from playing even though I'd given Len the same lessons.

After Len had seen me guide a set of darts into a tight cluster, he told me that throwing darts was easy. He threw the first dart like a baseball and hit the board an inch from the edge. "You throw like somebody cut your dick off," he said, and I moved back another step as he wound up again. There were six darts, and four of them missed the board, three of those four sticking outside the corkboard safety square that added six inches to protect the wall. "This game sucks," Len said. "These darts are too little," and he yanked them out and stuck them back into the center of the board while I touched each one of those holes as if I could repair them with fingerprints.

After he inspected the holes, my father said I should understand that Len Shambach was so squirrelly he was likely to get himself killed along with whoever was close by. My father believed he saw things clearly that way. He worked in an office for a company that made cameras and film. He "kept the books" is how he put it, just one right way and one right way only to do that job, and he never elaborated. "You can't have him in the basement," my father said. "Not now. Not ever."

Not ever was about how long it would be before I told my father about Len's tantrum box, a five-foot cube of padded wood that sat in the corner of Len's bedroom like a dog house. Len told me he'd been using that box since he was seven. "I always take my glasses off before I get in," Len said. "I used to scream while I kicked and punched it inside. It felt really good, but I stopped that shit a year ago."

I'd been inside that box the one time Len's mother had picked me up and driven me there on a Sunday afternoon. After I crawled through what looked like a door for a mid-size dog, I saw it was padded with the stuff we tumbled on in gym class. I smacked the walls a few times, and it didn't feel good at all, but I was pretty sure that Len would soon break it if he went back to punching and kicking.

"It's weird," Len said. "Now I just flop down in there in the dark without my glasses, and it feels like I'm laying in soup or something."

THE WEATHER BROKE IN LATE JANUARY, and a sunny forty degrees for three straight days felt so much like spring that Len rode his bike into town and we walked the six blocks to the drug store where we bought Milky Ways before I followed him five blocks farther to where the railroad track ran perpendicular to Main Street. "Pleasant Street," Len said, as if we weren't standing underneath the sign where the street ended because the tracks and the creek they followed curved around the edge of town on the other side of Main before straightening and going south into farm land. "It's like a local joke here," he said, beginning to walk. There was a beauty shop, a bar, a crushed cinder alleyway, and then four blocks of mostly boarded up houses facing the tracks that ran down the opposite side instead of a sidewalk. Almost every house had a lopsided porch that sagged right up against the sidewalk, the back yards drifted into dunes that were pocked where blackberry vines and sumac were poking through the receding snow. By the time we'd covered two blocks, those abandoned houses reminded me of decayed teeth because in among them were three or four houses that still had lights on, a space shoveled out from their front doors down the porch steps to where the sidewalk was plowed in one straight strip that still looked crisp even though the sides were less than knee deep now. At the end of the four blocks the street went on for ten feet into the woods before the plowed snow heaved up head high, the cracked asphalt spreading past the last house as if the pavers needed to dump and flatten the rest of a load instead of using it someplace else.

That night, at dinner, when I asked my father if he'd ever driven down Pleasant Street, he looked grim. "There's another fellow at work who lives out this way, and he tells me that street was never pleasant," he said, "not even when the company that owned the old factory across the creek built them so everybody could live nearby and walk to work. There was a footbridge until the town took it down a few years back. They made industrial springs there, shipped them out by train until they went bust after the war. They named it Pleasant Street like that would make that neighborhood a place where anybody except the desperate would live."

"Why do you say they were desperate?" my mother asked, and my father looked at her as if she'd tossed a dart into the basement wall.

"Cheryl," he said, but then he picked up a slice of bread, buttered it, and stuffed half of it into his mouth.

"LET'S LOOK FOR SECRETS," Len said when practice ended twenty minutes early one afternoon in mid-February.

"What secrets?" I said, but he was already walking toward the gate near the gym that was locked by the janitor around 5:30 every day to keep students from roaming the halls.

"Stuff teachers write down. Anything we're not supposed to know." He tugged the gate, and it slid open. "See?" he said. "Old man Schwartz won't come by here for almost half an hour."

I tagged along as Len tried each door on the first floor, every one locked but the bathrooms. I thought he'd give up then and go outside like he was supposed to and wait for his mother, but he opened the girls' room door, and I was sure I had to follow or listen to him call me names from inside like he'd found something special. The bathroom had six stalls, three sinks, and dispensers for paper towels and feminine napkins. I was afraid to even whisper, but Len didn't talk either. He stood on a seat and slipped aside a panel of the stained false ceiling, then another, as if he wanted to leave some sign of entry, receiving a brief, scattered shower of what I thought must be asbestos, that miracle we'd just studied in science, both of us getting As on our tests.

A few seconds later Len reopened the door so cautiously I was worried he'd heard footsteps. "All clear," he said, and once we were in the hall and on our way back to the still-open gate I started imagining which girls might look up the next day, one of them unsettled enough, maybe, by seeing the hidden anatomy of the school, that she would climb up to put those panels back in place. She might even be in science class with us, and we'd know because she'd be brushing dust from her dark sweater, her breasts and shoulders collecting a mystery of particles, those flakes so much like dandruff she might look up at the ceiling as if she thought somebody, before she noticed the displaced panels, had been clinging to those pipes, that his eyes had been on her as she sat in that stall, memorizing her like a formula.

BASKETBALL ENDED. I'd started the last four games and held my own. Len got in when we were ahead or behind by fifteen points with a minute to go. The Russians, one day in early March, sent up and then recovered a dog named Chernushka.

"They have it down pat now," my father said. "They're cooking with gas. And we're still fiddling around. We don't have the get up and go like the Communists."

"That name means 'Blackie,'" my mother said. "Don't you think it's funny how Russians name their dogs the way children would. Next thing you know they'll call one Spot or even Puff like the kids did in those books that teach everybody how to read."

"The Communists don't name their children Dick and Jane," my father said.

"Why would they?" Bonnie said. "They don't read our schoolbooks."

"Don't you bet your allowance on it. They know everything we do. Before you know it, they'll be looking in your window."

"Donald," my mother said, "listen to yourself."

"Just you wait then. Come back and sit at this table in five years and tell me who's running the world."

"I won't be anywhere near here in five years," Bonnie said, gripping her fork as if it was a weapon.

My mother reached across the table and touched Bonnie's fork-filled hand. "Well, let's try to be happy while we can then."

LEN TOLD ME HE KNEW all about the dogs in space. "They use those huskies," he said. "They know everybody will think they're so cute and hope the rocket works."

All I knew were their names and they were alive, but when I got to the part about my father worrying about Communists, Len acted excited. "Your old man's right. My old man is all the time talking about how there's ways to work everything out, but as soon as the Russians have men in space they'll let us have it with both barrels. We should join the Marines as soon as we're old enough."

"Men will be in space way before that," I said.

"We'll have guns. We'll be better off than everybody back here sitting in some fucking algebra class when the bombs drop."

"Nobody will know the difference if that happens."

"Every last person won't be gone. We just have to make sure we end up in a lucky spot."

"The Marines are never in a lucky spot," I said, and Len made a pistol with one finger and his thumb, aimed it at my head, and quietly fired.

I told my father my social studies teacher had said what Len had told me. "Is that teacher of yours giving you a test on that?"

"No," I said, glad that he didn't ask for the teacher's name.

"One thing he's got right. For sure, the bomb won't drop here," my father said. "Look southeast or southwest for all that."

"It will be different living here afterwards," I said.

"It won't be different," he said. "It will be impossible."

DURING JANUARY AND FEBRUARY, I'd gone to two dances in the school gym and stood around listening to Len Shambach criticize ninth grade girls until his mother picked him up fifteen minutes before the dance was scheduled to end so she didn't have to sit, she said, "in a big line of cars." My sister went to these dances, but she left even earlier with a boy named Grant Hutchings, who played varsity basketball. Bonnie told me our father was right about Len. "Grant says stay away from that dipshit, or pretty soon everybody will think you're a dipshit too."

"Basketball's over and he rides the bus home, so I only see him at school."

"Like father, like son is what Grant says. That dipshit's father's a douche bag."

Easy for her, I told myself. She'd stopped complaining about moving after she started riding around in Grant Hutchings' car and going to parties at houses. On foot, I couldn't do anything else but go to movies in town. Nobody our age had parties at their houses, Len said, but "Just wait until we can drive. That's when real parties with booze start unless you go to one of those dumps on Pleasant Street." According to him there were real parties all the time in the abandoned houses on Pleasant Street, but they were filled with retards and scumbags who weren't even teenagers anymore, and the only way to get in was to know one of them. "Next time you talk to that whore you like and get her to invite us. We can fuck her when she's drunk."

The only person who lived on Pleasant Street that I'd talked to was Carol Scheuing, who, Len said, was an easy lay who had six older brothers and no father. "Who are you?" she'd said the week before in the hall.

"Donnie Rogers."

"Why don't I remember ever seeing you?"

"I just moved here in January."

"That's a long time already," she'd said. "Have you been hiding?"

And though that was the end of what she'd said, I had to admit I'd been wondering what Carol Schueing did when a vacant house on her block was filled with a few dozen losers, some of them in their twenties.

The next afternoon I watched Carol walk down the hall toward me. She had books in her hands. Her blouse was buttoned to the top like every other girl's. "Hey there," I said. "I'm still here." And then I held my breath as she slowed and looked me over.

"Donnie the new boy," she said. "You drink, don't you?"

"Sure," I lied.

"If I tell my brothers you're ok, for a dollar you get a cup you can fill until the beer's gone at 38 Pleasant Friday night."

"Thirty-eight," I repeated, happy to have a word I didn't choke on.

"You need to write it down?" Carol said, but she was smiling.

Friday night, instead of going into the movie theater, I headed toward Pleasant Street. "You really going?" Len said, walking beside me, and I wished I hadn't told him about the invitation. When I turned down Pleasant without answering, he whispered, "I bet you won't go in."

"I'm invited," I said. "I'll pay my dollar."

"The place will be full of whores."

"So, follow me in. Use your movie money."

All we did was walk around sipping beer for an hour. The three girls we saw looked older than Bonnie, and Len didn't mention the word *whore*. I knew that everybody who was our age spent half the day at the vocational training school. Nobody talked to us, but we both pissed in the bathtub like all the boys did, and the girls, we noticed, used an empty closet where somebody had put a red plastic bucket, their privacy protected by one of the other girls taking turns guarding the door.

I filled my cup twice, but I didn't think I was getting drunk. But the one toilet was full of vomit, dried and fresh, and I'd felt sure that somewhere near the bottom of that mess was month's old shit from way back when the water had first been turned off. And I had to imagine the furniture that had been there once from broken wooden spokes of wood and a few moldy cushions. Nothing was in one piece.

"There's your girl-friend," Len said as Carol came downstairs through a crowd. "I bet somebody was up there fucking her."

"Donnie Rogers and his faithful sidekick," Carol said. She drank from the cup she was carrying and looked at Len. "I know your father," she said, and then she turned, handed me her cup, and said, "Try this."

Whatever it was burned the whole way down my throat, and Carol laughed, taking the cup back. "You've never had vodka, have you?"

"No."

"One cup makes your head spin. It's not like beer." She took another sip and touched my arm. "Come on upstairs, and I'll get you some."

We went into a small room that seemed cleaner than the rest of the house, but it was vacant except for a mattress on the floor. "This used to be a little girl's room," Carol said. "I used to hang out here with her before she moved in fourth grade." She sat down on the mattress, looking to where Len hovered behind me.

"You have to leave," she said to Len. "This isn't some show."

Len punched my shoulder. "I'll be right outside," he said.

I sat beside Carol on the mattress and took another quick sip of the vodka while she took off her sweater. I felt like I was sweating inside my body, but I stayed fixed on Carol. Her bra had little flowers on it. Roses. "Well," she said. I put my hand on her breast as she unhooked the bra, and it draped over her hand, exposing the other breast. "Look at you," she said, reaching for my zipper. I watched as my jeans opened as if they belonged to someone else, and I came as soon as her hand brushed my penis.

"Wow," she said.

"I'm sorry," I said, and I reached into my jeans pocket for the handkerchief my mother made me carry.

"What for?"

"I don't know."

While I wiped myself off, she let me look at her breasts before she hooked the bra. "I saw you playing basketball one time. You're the tallest boy on the team."

"Second tallest."

"Really?"

"But he never plays."

"We can try this again, Donnie Rogers. My brothers won't hate you if I tell them not to."

Len was waiting in the hall drinking beer from his plastic cup. He looked past me to where Connie was picking up her sweater and pulling it over her head. "You fuck her?" he said, and I pushed past him.

"I'm getting a beer," I said.

"I think I'm too drunk to fuck her."

Carol was still sitting on the mattress looking at the doorway. "She's fat," Len said. "I never knew she was fat."

"She's not fat."

"I can't fuck a fat girl."

When that house and the one next door burned down a week later, my father said, "That's a start." Carol Scheuing, I could have told him, lived beside two vacant lots now.

Another dog went up and came back safely. Zvezdochka, the paper said, a white dog, and it had completed one orbit before it returned. "Little Star" was how the newspaper translated its name. "Still so childish," my mother said.

"Childish or not, that's two in one month," my father said. "It's any day now for a man to be up there."

THE NEXT NIGHT the weather went to hell, one last lake effect storm blowing in from Lake Ontario, made worse because the ice had melted. "April Fool's," Bonnie said in the morning. "It figures."

A guy from basketball, Corey Baylor, walked from where he lived two blocks away and spent the afternoon of our snow day shooting pool in our basement. My father, off from work as well because of the drifted snow, heard the balls clicking and came downstairs before we were finished with the first game of eight ball.

Corey won the game easily, running the last four balls, all of them simple shots because the cue ball seemed to end up where even Len Shambach would have made the shot. "Good," my father said. "Keep beating my boy until he learns that getting position is as important as making the shot."

When Corey left after winning nine out of eleven games, my sister said, "That's better," and my father, sitting in the living room, shouted "A-men." I didn't tell either of them that I'd promised Len Shambach I'd sleep over at his house that weekend because his parents had bought an extra ticket for an American League playoff hockey game at a college in Rochester.

LEN HARDLY TALKED WHILE WE RODE HOME from the game, and he shut up completely while we ate a pizza and watched a horror movie on television. As soon as the giant octopus was finally killed, Len took off his glasses and crawled into his tantrum box. "You going to sleep in there?" I said.

For a minute he didn't say anything, and I asked again whether he was coming out. This time he said, "I heard Corey Baylor shot pool with you on your old man's precious table."

"He walked over. He lives close."

"What?" Len said. "Baylor likes you because you're so cool now that you fucked Carol Schueing?"

I stuck my head in the little door and said, "I didn't do anything with her."

"Bullshit. Get your ass all the way in here and tell me that," he said, tugging at my arm and pulling. I was half way in when he said, "I saw her tits and everything, and she was right there on that mattress."

"We just talked."

"Fuck you. I hope you get one of those diseases and your dick falls off." Len got quiet, and I waited for an excuse to crawl back out. "I was never not by myself in here," he finally said.

"That's the idea, right?"

He didn't answer. There was room inside for both of us as long as we sat with our knees drawn up. I wanted to ask Len if the dark looked blurry, but I didn't. "It makes you feel like an animal in here, doesn't it?" he said.

"What kind?"

"Something little," Len said, pushing me, and I took it as a signal to slip back out. "Something nobody even knows is right there close to them." Len crawled out and put on his glasses. "Let's go to Pleasant Street. I'll ask Carol Scheuing and see what she says about your dick.

Then I'll fuck her too."

"That's a long walk in the middle of the night."

"Follow me if you aren't a pussy."

His parents were asleep. We walked through the kitchen, and Len picked up his father's keys where they lay in an unused ash tray by the phone. "You can't drive," I said, but Len muttered "pussy" as he opened the door, and I followed him outside. A few seconds later Len slipped off the emergency brake of his father's car and allowed it to drift down the Shambach's long driveway before he turned the key in the ignition and said, "Let's rock" as if I'd been in on the plan to drive the dark green Ford at one a.m.

I thought he'd drive slow, afraid to have anything happen, but we sped off and went through the stop sign at the end of the street, swerving onto the narrow two-lane that wound up the hill behind Len's house and led away from town and Pleasant Street. I braced myself against the dashboard and Len laughed. "Driving's easy," he said, though he was a few months younger than me, and so short, I realized that he had to sit up straight to see the road, holding the wheel at nine and three o'clock.

We made a mile before the car ran onto the shoulder, and Len overcorrected through the oncoming lane. He slammed on the brake just as we touched the loose gravel and ice patches of the opposite shoulder, the car skidding until it nosed over the hillside and floundered thirty feet through what was left of the three-day-old snowstorm. Wedged, finally, between two sturdy trees, the right side sank so deep into a drift that Len tumbled downand pressed me against the door.

Len turned off the engine and took his weight partially off me by grabbing the steering wheel. "We have to get out," he said. "My old man's going to kill us."

I couldn't push the door open more than a few inches. The power window wouldn't budge. "Turn the key," I said. "I need to get the window down." When Len twisted the key, I wound the window down and pushed my head and shoulders through as the car settled another few inches, the angle frightening now that I would be underneath the frame if it tipped.

"Hurry up," Len shouted, turning the key back to OFF, but I was being careful, squeezing my hips through the window before I let go and dropped into the snow. I was surprised how soft the landing was. The snow had drifted deep where the car was stuck. I thought there was a good chance the car would sink even further onto its side, and I scrambled clear of it just as Len let go of the wheel and tumbled against the window, banging his head on the frame. "Fuck," Len said, and then he set about worming through.

The snow soaked through the knees of my jeans, and I pushed myself to my feet, the snow half way up my calves. Len sat in a drift, and for once he didn't say anything about how cool it was to do something stupid. I moved to where the hood of the car was caught against the trunks of two birch trees. Aside from the angle at which it was tilted, the car appeared to be stable now, but when I looked past those trees I saw that there was a drop of at least fifty feet nearly straight down to where the moonlight reflected off a half-frozen creek that wound through rocks large enough to terrify. There were other trees growing near the edge of the cliff, but none within twenty feet of where I stood, and the closest ones looked thin enough for a car to snap off on its way over the brink.

Len came up beside me and peered down. "I used to play in that creek where it's closer to my house," he said. "Back before middle school when I didn't even know you. There's lots of frogs and salamanders and shit." I stepped away from the edge and figured the best way back up would be to follow the path the car had taken because it had plowed some of the snow ahead of it. "My old man's going to be super pissed at us," Len said as I began to climb. "I left the keys in the car. If we sneak into the house, maybe he'll think the car was stolen."

I wanted to sneak into a house, all right, but it was two miles away where my sister Bonnie and my parents were sleeping. When I started walking in the opposite direction, Len said, "You're part of this, Rogers," but I kept going, not even turning my head when Len shouted "Fuck you" six times as if he was emptying a gun at my back.

It took me almost an hour to walk home. My father was waiting in the living room when I came in the side door. "Len Shambach's father called to tell me you stole his car and wrecked it," he said. "Tell me why you got into that car with that boy."

"Len did all that."

"So, he's wrong about everything?"

"Mostly."

"That's better. You look like part of you is guilty as all get out. Your mother's sick with worrying."

"I knew Len was going to wreck. I was glad we went off the road before we got to where there's more traffic. I was happy while we slid down the hill. I didn't know there was a cliff."

"A cliff? Let's take a look." My father led me outside to his car and drove until I showed him the accident site. He slowed the car where the shoulder widened and swung the car into a slow arc until we were turned around. "Show me the cliff," he said.

The Ford was still there. "I imagine Mr. Shambach will be here any minute. A tow truck has to come," my father said. I was shivering now, the thin jacket I'd started wearing when March began because I thought it looked cool suddenly as stupid as riding with Len Shambach.

"Good, let them come," I said.

"Mr. Shambach can hear you tell your story then. I bet he knows how it went already."

I skidded down the hill behind my father, who stepped right to the edge of the cliff, holding on to one of the birch trees while he peered over the edge. "You be careful here," he said. "We don't need you falling after all the good luck you just had."

I placed my shoes into the prints I'd left an hour ago, but they seemed so close to the edge now that I backed up a step. "In two years, you'll have a driver's license," my father said without looking at me. "What then?"

"I'll be careful."

"No, you won't. When you're sixteen you'll think you're such hot shit you'll be embarrassed to drive at the speed limit."

"Bonnie will be driving this summer," I said. "What then?"

"Bonnie's a girl. She has other things to worry me with." The white cloud of my father's breath was so close to mine that they seemed to mix. We stood beside each other for a few more seconds, and then my father looked up. "Some cosmonaut, whoever he's going to be, could be taking off right this minute," he said. "Whoever he is, he'll have some ride."

"You know what Mr. Shambach said tonight when I told him that the Russians were going to have the first man in space?" I said. "'The sky isn't falling, young Rogers."

My father kept looking up as if he hadn't heard me. "It's smaller than you think, that spaceship. A man's got to feel it's not up to him what happens in a thing like that."

"Len told his dad you thought the world would end when the Russians put a man up there, and I didn't know what to say."

My father gripped my shoulders as if he believed I might stumble backwards over the edge. "In less than two years there will be all sorts of men in space," he said, "and you'll be driving like every boy does who just happens to be your age."

I pulled away, but I held the birch's trunk, looking down at the distant creek. "The phone will ring and your mother will get out of bed and answer. She'll say come out here and hear this. Someone's just told me our son's gone over a cliff in our car."

I let go of the tree and held my ground. My father moved so close that our shoulders touched. "You know what I'll say if you're not dead when I see you?" he said. "Begin at the very start and tell me the truth." Because I thought he expected me to speak, I used a few seconds to open my stance as if I needed to balance myself in the snow. I swallowed hard then. I concentrated on making sure my voice would be steady and turned toward him, but he was still looking at the sky, and I didn't have to do anything but stand beside him and wait until he was finished staring.

The World Without Us

MY WIFE KATHLEEN DESIGNS COATS for the cancer stricken. Something comfortable, she says, for the unfortunate to wear during chemotherapy sessions. When a reporter interviewed her for the local paper two months ago, her friend Annie modeled them for the photo the paper ran with the article. Despite her diagnosis, Annie looked healthy. She gave a remission smile. The reporter allowed Kathleen to post the unused photos on her web site that features a video made at the chemo center. Annie sits among several other patients and says a few lines about how the coat is warm but not bulky, that it somehow feels natural to be wearing one indoors. The other patients had given permission to have their identities as cancer patients revealed.

Maybe not so surprising, Annie's willingness to promote. Even under her circumstances, she's a go-getter, smoothing the way with the other patients, one of whom bought a coat on the spot. But the first thing I noticed when I watched the video was the patient who looked to be in her 20s, a beauty who, Kathleen said, had just been told she had a brain tumor after a year of being treated for migraines. What I didn't tell Kathleen was I think there's cooperation from the patients because my wife, like me, is nearly seventy, and maybe those patients aren't put off by someone with a limited future.

I used to tell her we're all balloons in that old carnival dart game, even if we're underinflated and way up in the corner, the balloons nobody aims at. "You're always so downbeat," she'd say. "All you have are conditions that are monitored like anybody our age. Arthritis, cataracts, skin cancer, a couple of kidney stones. All that adds up to is nothing but maintenance."

There's truth in that, for certain, because she's the one who is dying, though not of cancer, not the horror she'd conditioned herself to accept when it arrived. All those coats. All those patients, especially the ones who were younger than herself. They had been enough to show her inevitability and the best ways to deal with it.

But here, with last month's diagnosis of oncoming dementia, there isn't any operation or chemo or hair loss, there's only each day more confusing than the last, the increments so tiny she won't even notice them until some accident or embarrassment announces the advance of damage. For now, the evidence is private, the sticky notes reminding her of things a child would do automatically. The careful arranging of medicines. The calendar thick with events that are annotated with explanations.

She wants to go on trips. New places are good for the brain, she says. We'll start with places close by until we agree on a faraway place we both want to go to. She has promised herself not to be bitter.

WE STARTED WITH THE HOLOCAUST MUSEUM, a couple of hundred miles to drive, and neither of us ever there all these years. I told her not to turn Siri on like she does now for just about any place but where we can walk to, and she fidgeted even when we could see the Washington Monument clear as day and getting clearer by the block.

But when there was a detour, I ended up on a one-way street with the Monument in the rearview mirror, and she had Siri on in a heartbeat, pronouncing Holocaust Museum like a child sounding out a new word. It's like eyes, she said. It tells you what you can't see. Why not listen?

The parking lot was full of school buses, the museum crowded with middle school kids who flitted from one thing to another. "Those kids won't remember anything except what they had for lunch," Kathleen said, "but even when things get worse, I'll remember all of those dead peoples' shoes they had piled up. Something like that will never go dark."

TWO WEEKS AGO, FOR MY FIRST TURN, I took us two hundred miles another direction to Pittsburgh. "Absolutely no Siri," I said when we were on the Parkway East heading toward the city.

"Let's hope not. This isn't new like I want. We've been here a bunch of times already," she said, but when I turned at the Homestead exit, she sighed. "Well, ok, I haven't been here, but you know all this because you grew up just down the road."

"It's all new since I left. It's brand new for you."

The town was still there, but now even a number of churches were for sale, the businesses closed, the houses crumbling. When Kathleen went quiet, I wondered whether I'd picked a terrible place because she saw Homestead as an omen, all the old people who looked across the railroad tracks to where the world's largest steel mill had stood and were surprised the neighborhood they'd known had disappeared. Whether they were afraid to leave the town because everything else might have vanished as well, a kind of Shangri-la in reverse, everything in their lives aging while the rest of the world stayed new.

She complained when we sat in Eat 'n Park where there wasn't an item on the menu she'd never had before. "It's just eggs and toast and coffee," she said. "I'll be able to remember breakfast when I can't recognize our next-door neighbors."

I didn't say anything, but when we left, I had her look at the photographs on the wall in the lobby, the old black-and-whites that announced how enormous the mill was right where, once we were outside, I waved my arm around like a guide. Apartments, condominiums, Target, Lowe's, Costco, Giant Eagle, a movie multiplex, franchise restaurants, and closest to the river, a waterslide park called Sandcastle. "That mill covered all of this," I said, standing beside a preserved, enormous steel beam and coil, memories so shiny and clean they looked as artificial as the perfect brick smokestacks outside the Longhorn Steakhouse.

"This feels like the future," Kathleen said.

"It's ok. You didn't live in Homestead."

"I'm not talking about the town. All it did was get old."

"Up the Ohio, in Aliquippa, nobody's even done anything except level the mill and cart everything away. There's nothing at all."

"I don't need to see that," she said.

The day after Homestead I had my cataracts appointment to keep. After my pupils were dilated, all I learned was that it would be another year before the doctor would think seriously about removal.

Kathleen drove us the eight miles home. Neither of us said a word about whether or not she'd be driving me after those cataracts were removed. It was so sunny, the world sparkled even when I squinted behind dark glasses, so I closed my eyes until the car turned left way before it was supposed to.

"A lot of traffic?" I said, my eyes still closed.

"A lot of stop signs."

I opened my eyes slightly and squinted. Stopped at an intersection, Kathleen was fumbling with her phone. "Where are we?" I said.

"I don't know," she said. "I've never been here before. I need to ask Siri." From behind us, a horn blew.

"Don't bother with that," I said. "Turn left again. And don't worry about that asshole."

Kathleen turned, and because we were facing away from the sun, I could make something out if I stayed squinted. "Turn left again," I said, and two blocks later, "Now turn right." Ahead of us was a sign directing us to turn right again to reach the road we always use.

"Thank God," Kathleen said, and I closed my eyes again, keeping them shut when I felt us winding through the access ramp to the bridge a half mile from our street and even until we stopped in our driveway, doing what I could to calm her.

But when we were back inside our house, Kathleen began to cry. "Your clouds will go away," she said. "Mine are getting thicker." Her voice trailed off and then returned. "I hate self-pity, but I never thought I'd go crazy."

"You're not insane."

"Yes, I am. I'm somebody else part of the time now. Like Eve, the three faces one, not the naked girl in the garden."

"We watched that movie twenty years ago on television. Joanne Woodward was three sides of Eve."

"Paul Newman's wife," she said. "I remember everything I don't need to know."

"All of it is important," I said, but she looked as if she'd drifted, a vacancy in her expression that was more unsettling than an open-mouthed gasp of pain. She sat down on the couch, the movement slow and careful. Like the very old, I thought. Like the fragile. When she settled, she looked at me and smiled as if I'd just entered the room. "Just think," she said. "I was always terrified of losing a breast."

It's turned out people buy those coats. "Because they're made of hope," Kathleen says, and for once I agree because Kathleen seems sharper when she's working with the coats, so much so, that when she's excited about them I'm able to think that every once in a long while, somebody comes back from the brink, a miracle that lets us believe we could be the ones who will be blessed like those passengers standing on the wings of the plane Sully landed on the Hudson River. Anything's possible, that makes us think. We might even pay attention to the "in case of a water landing" instructions before takeoff over the ocean.

Kathleen has always been one of those who listens to the flight attendant explain emergency response, how the aisle has lights to guide us, how there are multiple exits, perhaps one close behind us. She always turns to check while I work the crossword puzzle in the airline magazine to calm my nerves and try to ignore that line about the seat cushion becoming a flotation device. Yet she doesn't believe in God, not one bit, even though he has a better chance of existing than anybody who is part of a water landing in the middle of the ocean.

When I Google Sully, I find a miracle I remember from when we were first married. The pilot was young, the hatch blown open. It happened the week of our honeymoon when we hadn't watched television or read a newspaper. I locate the pilot's interview, how he admitted that he'd already thought about how he faced a lifetime of never having to be as skillful. Like an athlete, he said, like somebody who'd managed an extraordinary play that would never happen again.

WHEN KATHLEEN PICKED PENN'S CAVE LAST WEEK because it's only an hour's drive, I worried that the radius of our trips had already begun to shrink. She said it was because we'd ride on a boat way down inside it, that neither of us had even been in any kind of cave. She started Siri as soon as we got in the car.

In the cave she seemed fine, her gaze moving from stalactite to stalagmite

Like an ordinary tourist. Maybe, I thought, this thing will move slowly, that we'll have a few more years of small failures before I need to master the behavior finality requires. Responses. Reactions. Readiness. A sort of three Rs for the return trip to elementary school. And beyond.

"Look at that," she said of a suggestive formation spotlighted by the guide. "It looks like a wall in God's wine cellar," and her ease into simile brought up a surge of joy into my throat.

"Or like the shelves in Satan's pub," I said, and Kathleen laughed like she always has, high–pitched and politely stifled to keep from bothering anyone in the boat.

AT THE GROCERY STORE THIS MORNING Kathleen says, "Look there" and tugs me up beside her while she calls out "Hello."

"Well, hello there, you two," a woman says, and I recognize her—Annie from the photo shoot. She has nothing but produce in her small cart.

"You have one of my coats," Kathleen says. "I'd know that from a mile away."

"It's as good as advertised," Annie says.

"I'm glad you like it," Kathleen says, her expression so neutral I begin to sweat.

Annie glances at her kale and tomatoes, fixed on them. "You should know I've had a setback since the video. Thirteen good months. I have to think of them as a gift."

I wait for Kathleen to say there could be another gift, remission still possible even if temporary, but she says, "Gifts are always good."

"There's never enough," Annie says, but Kathleen is already pushing our cart past her, and I am left to smile and shrug.

As soon as we turn into an aisle of frozen foods, Kathleen whispers, "I knew she was going to stop and talk, but I couldn't remember who that was. And then she was gone and her name came to me just now."

This afternoon, preparing for a trip to the post office, Kathleen says, "I can't find my keys."

"Borrow mine. You don't need them."

"Yes, I do," she says, suddenly angry. "You wouldn't leave without your own keys."

It takes ten minutes of eliminating places, including the laundry hamper and every couch and chair cushion before, in a rage, Kathleen flings open the refrigerator to retrieve the Brita pitcher and sees the keys lying on the shelf beneath it. "My God," she says. "Oh, Jesus Christ."

"I've left mine in worse places," I say, but no particular location comes to me.

"Take these," she says, handing me the chilled keys. "You go. I can't. Not now."

And I do, saying nothing. I take my time with the package and the insurance, and when I get home, Kathleen's reading a book, composed.

"Promise me you won't be afraid of me," she says at once. "That you won't talk to me like you're a hostage."

"Don't worry," I say, but she closes her book and lays it on her lap as if she's embarrassed. "You know what terrifies me? That people will only remember who I'll be, that I'll stay like that for so long people will forget."

"I won't."

"Then tell people stories with places and people in them when they ask about me, not the funeral words like kind and generous."

Tonight, both of us in bed, Kathleen says, "I'm not in pain. Here I am coming apart, and I don't even feel it inside."

"For sure, there's worse."

"No, there's not. Annie will be herself almost until the day she dies. I'll be something else for years and years. A zombie." She takes a breath and looks away.

"I've been reading that book that was made into a movie about the early-onset woman. She wanted to kill herself before she turned. Just like when somebody gets bitten in The Walking Dead."

"That's because those zombies are dangerous."

She turns away from me so fast, I shudder. "Don't you think having me around won't kill you too?"

She lies facing away like that until I turn off the light. "Pick a place neither of us has ever seen before this time. Make sure I don't think I've forgotten something."

"I already did," I say. "You'll see. I won't say anything until we're almost there. Just trust me."

I shut up then, saying nothing about the miles-long stretch of abandoned Pennsylvania Turnpike I've read about, the no-longer-used tunnels you can walk through if you have the nerve and a reliable flashlight, tunnels that were closed in the late 1960s because they were only one lane wide each way on a four-lane expressway, tunnels that forced an alternate way over the mountains to be constructed.

And then she turns back to face me. "This will be the last time for driving," she says. "We need to begin going to the far-away," and I feel my body go hot.

The turnoff near Breezewood is right where the web site had promised it would be. For two hours, Kathleen has been silent, but now she sits up, expectant, but it's only a hundred yards or so before the road forks, and nothing I've read has given me a clue for making a choice.

"Left or right?" I say.

"There's no telling," Kathleen says. "What are we doing out here?" I swing to the left and start downhill on the quickly narrowing road, and she points out a No Trespassing sign. "We're in slasher movie territory," I say.

"Turn around," she says, and when I don't stop, she adds, "Now."

A quarter mile later, the forest thick on both sides and steeply falling away on our right, Kathleen nods toward a second, more ominous hand-painted No Trespassing sign. I begin to consider more realistic scenarios, all of them including vicious dogs and a recluse with an arsenal.

When I stop and make my first tiny swing, Kathleen, without my asking, gets out and signals how close I am to the ditch. She moves to the rear and waves me past where I was sure the shoulder ended. Then again. Then again, before she opens the door and climbs back in. "I still have the common sense in this family," she says. It feels good to see, two minutes later, an ordinary pickup truck appearing from the other road.

We follow that road a few miles, the active turnpike we've just left revealing itself to our right. Shortly after it vanishes, I spy, through the forest to our left, what looks to be the abandoned road. A hundred yards later there is a small parking area empty of cars. "There's a lost turnpike right over there," I say. "Miles of it, and lost tunnels, too, because they used old one-lane railroad tunnels instead of building new ones here."

"So, we're hiking where we've never been?" Kathleen says. "On a closed road?" She reaches into the back seat and produces two of her cancer coats. "It's not as warm as you think," she says. "Not if we're out in the woods like this." When she places one in my hands, she says, "Something brand new for you. Maybe this will help you appreciate how lucky you are not being hooked up to that poison at the center."

What looks like a path is so over grown I suspect we're parked in the wrong place for exploring, but Kathleen takes the lead as if she's in a hurry, so sure-footed I feel myself aging as I struggle. "Creepy," Kathleen says, when we stand on what once had been a heavily-traveled road, and I have to agree. Except for the pickup truck, we haven't seen anyone for so long it feels as if we've entered an alternate, uninhabited world. Or worse, and more likely, one so isolated and forgotten that whoever might show up wouldn't be someone we'd welcome.

"There's bears here, I bet," she says.

"We're in the open. We'll see anything a long way off."

"And everything will see us first."

"This is the Fordlandia of Pennsylvania," I say.

"And that means what?"

"Ford built a model town in the Amazon jungle way back when without listening to anybody who knew better. It's a ruin now, mostly, like this."

"It's not the same at all. This got left behind because the rest of the road worked so well they needed more lanes."

"In another forty years, when cars are obsolete, the whole turnpike will be like this."

Kathleen frowns. "Nothing's easier than predicting the future for a time when you're dead."

The asphalt is crumbling. The familiar milkweed. goldenrod, and burdock are waist high where cars once traveled. A few sumac trees ten feet tall are accelerating the split in the pavement. As far as we can see in either direction there is no one, and yet we are standing in the middle of what had once been the busiest highway in Pennsylvania. "Even the bears are gone," I say, but Kathleen doesn't smile.

"My father drove us through the tunnels one Sunday afternoon after he heard they were closing. I was a freshman in college and he made me get in the car. 'Once in a lifetime,' he said. "Turns out he was right."

"So, you cheated," Kathleen says. "You've seen this before."

"It's totally different."

Kathleen squints in both directions and turns as if she's going back to the car. "I pick Iceland for our next trip."

"What?"

"I want to go to Iceland. It has volcanoes and hot springs and everything absolutely new."

"It's October. I thought you'd pick some place tropical," I say. "You've always wanted to live where it's warmer."

"Either you don't get it, or you don't care. We've been in warm places in winter, but we've never been anywhere at any time of year like Iceland."

"We've never been any place like this road," I say. "This is the world without us,"

"No, it isn't," Kathleen says. "The real turnpike will still be up and running and the same as ever."

"I mean none of us. Everybody."

"You can't think that way. There's nothing but darkness there."

"I think of it every day."

"That's so selfish. Just because you'll be dead, you want everybody to be dead," Kathleen says. "You don't have any empathy."

"When it's earned, I do."

"There," Kathleen says. "And you don't even realize." She begins to cry. I think of embracing her, but now the gesture would seem as if I were reacting to her accusation.

She uses her little fingers to wipe the corners of her eyes. "I remembered something just now," she says. "From a long time ago. What my mother said about my father when I asked her about his racism, how he used all the worst words for everybody who wasn't white—'Otherwise, a good man.'" Her eyes focus on where the overgrown path begins as if she doesn't expect me to speak. "Have you had enough," she says.

"I want to see inside the tunnel," I say. "It's like not seeing the Mona Lisa if you go to the Louvre."

"You go. I already know what a mess looks like. I'll sit in the car and read."

"I thought you were nervous."

"The doors will be locked. The bears don't have a key."

"Fifteen minutes?"

"Twenty," she says. "Take your time." Her voice is as distant as the active turnpike's traffic noise. If you didn't have your cataracts, you could see the tunnel to the east of here from where we're standing, and I'll be hunkered down so far the boogie man will think we're both looking inside that tunnel."

"Twenty minutes," I say.

"But first follow me back to the car and let's get you a flashlight. You'll need one or else you won't see anything but a postcard."

THE TUNNEL, IT TURNS OUT, is less than two hundred yards away. Close enough to start jogging after a hundred yards, the asphalt broken and crushed into near-sand, easier on my knees than if it were new. The trees aren't yet in full color, but the sumac that has pushed up through cracks in the highway has already nearly finished dropping its red leaves, mixing with a scattering of maples and locust.

The entrance is so crowded with graffiti that ranges from romantic to violent that I think it's been years since anyone found room there to declare their love or hate. Once inside, I can see a light in the distance just like I'd read about in a blog. Ambient, the blogger had said, something like that, because it couldn't possibly be the real light from the other end a mile away.

I flick on the flashlight, but it doesn't have the same effect as headlights on a car. The light doesn't penetrate more than a step or two in front of me, and when I focus it on the ground, looking down at my feet, I feel light-headed from my hundred-yard jog. Cataracts don't matter here. The surface is so haphazardly littered, everybody needs to be cautious.

In less than a minute, as my light begins to dim and flicker, I wonder how long the batteries have been in a flashlight Kathleen and I use maybe twice a year. As it goes out, I remind myself the tunnel is wide and straight. All I have to do is not panic like I've done every time I've played blind on my sidewalk or on my stairs since the cataract diagnosis. Take ten steps forward, I think. Prove something to yourself, then turn around and go back to Kathleen.

I only stumble twice, but my breath turns labored. Ok, I think, there you are, then turn, my right shoulder glancing off the wall. Startled, I twist away from contact, one shoe stepping on a bottle, and I fall, the flashlight smacking against the road and tumbling into silence.

I lie on the asphalt for a few seconds, evaluating. None of my pain feels excruciating. I sit up, and then stand, staggering for a moment, pivoting to take the weight off my left knee, which flares into a pain not quite incapacitating. Ok, I say aloud, you can walk, though my right wrist aches as well, and I sense a throbbing begin in my shoulders and neck.

Knowing I'd struck the wall to my right, I reach with my right arm, but touch nothing. I sidestep twice and then a third time before I touch something solid. And though I know it's impossible, I consider the chance that I might set out in the wrong direction. I remember the flashlight flung into the darkness, but I don't want to spend time bent over and feeling around.

I hear voices, but don't see any lights. Who would be coming through in the dark? Teenagers? Kids drinking from six packs and tossing their empties? I expect the sound of cans clanging off the walls followed by laughter. I limp more quickly toward the light. The voices go quiet and then, after a few more steps, I hear them again, not any closer, but one of them a child's.

A light comes on behind me, and the child's voice squeals. Not for seeing me, I decide, pushing myself. It seems important not to be overtaken by a child and whoever is with her. A father most likely, a man who would, by now, be keeping an eye on me, measuring his steps so there was always some distance between us. Someone who might have questions for me once we were out of the tunnel. But after I limp a few steps away from the tunnel and look back, no one is visible.

I EXPECT TO SEE NOTHING CHANGED AT THE CAR, but there are two red canvas folding chairs sitting beside it. Good, I think, nothing has spooked her. She's inside watching me limping and will ask where the flashlight is, and I'll tell the story. She'll tell me she put the chairs out so we could sit in the sun a few minutes and how absorbed she was in the book, the multi-volume *My Life* or whatever it was called that Kathleen had started a year ago. She'd finished three volumes, coming back to the epic for an hour each night before sleep, as if it were literary warm milk, maybe only the one volume left to finish. Though who knew how many more that long-winded Norwegian would put out.

The book is lying open on a chair, the pages flapping in the wind, but Kathleen is gone. I stare in every direction, and then sweep the edge of the forest a second time before I open the door and blow the horn.

Before I move or call, she reappears a hundred feet away, stepping out of the trees nearest the active turnpike. "I had to pee so bad," she calls out as she gets closer. "There was no holding it another minute. It was like the old days at a keg party when the girls would circle up in the woods and you'd squat in the middle. But I got turned around in there far enough to feel safe and walked off the wrong way somehow."

"Jesus, this isn't the county park."

"But here I am right back where I started. You made such a racket with that horn. You could have called my name."

"The horn's louder."

She picks up the book. "I lost my place now with all the ruckus." She closes the book and opens it again. "You were gone forever. Wherever did you go?"

"The tunnel. You said it wasn't far."

"Did I now?"

"I'd be gone twenty minutes, tops. That's why you were alone in the car."

"And nearly peed my pants. What kind of tunnel is way out here?"

A truck horn wails through the trees. In the winter, I think, you could see the traffic from here. And maybe you could be seen from the highway. "I'll buy us tickets tomorrow," I say in what I hope is a jaunty voice. "We'll be on our way to Iceland before it gets too cold there."

"Iceland? Whatever for? It's so far." The locust buzz of my tinnitus is so insistent that I have to fight off the urge to turn around once to look behind me, afraid that I can't hear what might be coming. "Whatever are you talking about?" Kathleen says, but her voice, now, is anxious, her face tightening. I give her time. "Wherever have you been?" she says at last. "That coat is scuffed along the arm. Did you have some trouble?"

"Yes," I say, and hold my breath as if the sound of it might attract something terrible.

"You didn't have to go so far into the woods to pee. There's nobody here."

She looks down at the book as if she's reading from whatever page it's open to. "Or did you have to do more than pee and you couldn't find a good spot?" She pats one of the red chairs. "You look like you could use a rest," she says, and without speaking, I examine her expression.

"Maybe a short one."

"Maybe? I was sitting out here so long I felt like a widow."

"Iceland," I say again. "Volcanoes and hot springs and a world of difference."

Kathleen closes the book and blinks. "Wow," she says. "Just wow, oh wow. For a minute there, I forgot myself." She pats the chair again and says, "Sit."

For a moment, I feel afraid that she's turned a corner into a new level of darkness, and the I feel calmer than I have for weeks, maybe longer, a calmness that seems to come from finality, one more thing I won't be able to explain to her, how, when what I'd feared had finally occurred, I relaxed.

"You were right," she says, "not one person came by. The world without us isn't so bad, is it?" She sweeps one arm in an arc, inviting me to take in the landscape.

"I twisted my ankle and wrenched my knee," I say. "It took me forever to make my way back."

"But now you're here," she says. "Tell me everything. Tell me what you saw."

ACKNOWLEDGMENTS

Nothing Falls from Nowhere
(as "Things that Fall from the Sky")   *Green Mountains Review*

The Faces of Christ   *Southern Indiana Review*

Delightful Conversation   *Green Hills Literary Lantern*

Real Talking   *South Dakota Review*

See What I See   *South Carolina Review*

Human Subject   *Cheat River Review*

Flying to Alaska   *Blue Mesa Review*

The Eternal Language of the Hands   *Sonora Review*

Mothering   *Ascent*

The Variance   *Florida Review*

Dogs in Space   *South Carolina Review*

The World Without Us   *Valparaiso Fiction Review*

Flying to Alaska was reprinted in *The Best of Blue Mesa Review*